T0065230

GREY WOLF
and
ROSE

WILLIAM STANLEY

Archway Publishing books may be ordered
through booksellers or by contacting:

Archway Publishing
1663 Liberty Drive
Bloomington, IN 47403
www.archwaypublishing.com
844-669-3957

ISBN: 978-1-6657-5410-1 (sc)
ISBN: 978-1-6657-5411-8 (e)

Library of Congress Control Number: 2023923425

Print information available on the last page.

Archway Publishing rev. date: 12/11/2023

DEDICATION

This book is dedicated to the men and women who worked as fur trappers in an unforgiving land in the late nineteenth century. Their courage and perseverance led to recognition of this territory, known as the Yukon, in Canada's far north.

INTRODUCTION

Grey Wolf and Rose is the continuing story of the adventures of early fur traders who settled in a forest wilderness located in the Yukon. Recently married natives wishing to escape the confines of their tribe, they accept an offer from a virtual stranger which they could not refuse, a fully equipped cabin in the bush for their taking. This arrangement launches the couple into an adventure of love and commitment, living in the woods with the support of extended family members.

CHAPTER ONE

The howl of a lone wolf broke the silence of the dark forest. Grey Wolf and Rose sat outside their cabin, which Joe and Mary had so kindly given them. Grey Wolf stoked the campfire, adding more wood to the dying embers.

The young couple had arrived at Joe and Mary's cabin three days ago and were taken to their new home in the forest by the young couple. With a twenty-dollar gold piece Joe and Mary had given them, they had purchased supplies they needed for their new home. Grey Wolf had hired Bev's friend to pack in the goods they had purchased in Dawson yesterday, which would be arriving by mule tomorrow.

Summer had arrived in the Yukon. After a harsh winter, the trees were now covered in a green canopy, a coat they would not wear long. The vibrant meadows were full of birds and wildflowers, as well as numerous bees feasting on the sweet nectar of the colorful blossoms. The night was gripped in solitude, only the occasional soulful call of the loon could be heard coming from the lake.

Grey Wolf and Rose were experienced hunters, both raised in a tribe which lived on what food they could harvest from the forest. Rose was an only child, her mother having died from a disease brought to the Yukon by white men who came north looking for gold and fur. Her father taught her survival skills, educating Rose on where to find the bounty of food nature provided from the forests. He taught Rose how to hunt and sight a rifle when shooting at prey. Accuracy is critical when shooting a moose, as a misguided shot means the animal escapes and the hunter goes hungry.

During his latter years, Rose's father developed a drinking problem. He died at the hands of a white man, fighting over liquor for his fur in Dawson City. Still a teenage girl, Rose was taken in by Grey Wolf's parents. Over the years, Grey Wolf and Rose became inseparable and were married at their tribal camp when they were both twenty-one, before going to Dawson City to see Bev, an elder from their tribe and Rose's aunt.

Living in a cabin in the wilderness would be a huge challenge for Grey Wolf and Rose, but combining their knowledge of the bush should make their venture a success. Extended members of Bev's family, including Joe and Mary, would help this young couple in their times of need. The families who made up this clan in the forest also donated traps to the young couple, sparing them the expense of buying new ones. Grey Wolf and Rose had both trapped fur with their fathers, gaining valuable experience they would soon use as young adults.

The night was getting late, as the campfire burned down to the coals. A happy lifestyle was beginning for Grey Wolf and Rose, a beginning the couple had both prayed for.

CHAPTER TWO

G rey Wolf and Rose's new cabin was situated a half-a-day's walk from a town in chaos. Thousands of men and women had flooded into Dawson City, turning the growing city into a sea of debauchery. Gambling, drinking, and prostitution were favorite ways for these men to while away their time and spend their money. Drunks, lying passed out in the streets of mud, often had their heads stepped on, pushing their faces deep into the muck full of feces and urine. The city, having nowhere to rid itself of its waste, ended up with sewage and horse manure in the streets. Rain turned this sludge into a toxic brew with a horrible stench, which caused disease to spread. Instead of finding gold in the Yukon, the early prospectors found only death and despair, either by the hand of nature or at the end of a gun barrel of one of their fellow man. Grey Wolf and Rose had no interest in finding gold. The couple planned to make money trapping fur during the winter months.

A voice, yelling out a friendly, "Hello!", broke the stillness of the morning. Grey Wolf and Rose had previously met Steward at Bev's house in Dawson. After learning Steward raised dogs, they had told him they were interested in buying a husky, which would make a devoted pet. Steward had replied he had just the dog for the couple and would bring him to them in the future. Today he had traveled to their home via canoe, having left his cabin at daybreak.

Grey Wolf opened his door to a smiling Steward and a beautiful young husky named Charlie. The dog was a one-year-old male, who was friendly and loved the company of people. Steward gifted the dog to the young couple, knowing they were just starting out in life and had little money. Charlie was happy to have found a new home, where he would be treated like a pet and not a working dog. Grey Wolf told Steward his father was providing him with a dog team before winter, but he was elated to have a dog as a companion now.

Old Joe, who had previously owned the cabin Grey Wolf and Rose now called home, had kept dogs. However, the yard and dog houses were in rough shape due to years of neglect. Steward offered to help Grey Wolf fix up the yard and structures his sled team would call home. Grey Wolf graciously accepted Steward's offer of help, telling him when he was ready to do the work he would let Steward know. Steward and his wife, Blossom, were two of Grey Wolf's neighbours, living about two hours away from their cabin by water or dogsled. The couples would become good friends and helpful neighbours to each other in the future.

Charlie adapted right away to his new home, finding himself a comfortable spot by the woodstove to sleep. He was ready for the first cold temperatures of the season, when the couple would use the stove to heat the cabin. Then, Charlie, like many other dogs, would lie by the stove letting the heat warm his cold body. Few dogs enjoyed this luxury while living in the bush, as most dogs in the Yukon were used for work and not treated as personal pets. Charlie was an exception, getting to enjoy a good life compared to the sled dogs who were forced to live outside and sleep in the snow.

The cabin's previous owner had left behind a canoe when he died. A fine birch bark canoe, built by Old Joe's native friend twenty years ago, lay under a large tree, which sheltered the craft from the elements of nature. The condition of this craft was just like new. Old Joe had taken good care of his canoe, realizing how important it was for his survival.

After Steward left, the couple decided to take the canoe on the lake and fish the cold water for trout for dinner. The appeal of this solitary life was starting to grow on Grey Wolf and Rose. They were enjoying the pleasures of living in a land that offered the spirit so much joy but the body so little, a land they called the Yukon.

CHAPTER THREE

Grey Wolf and Rose pulled the canoe out from under the evergreen, where it had been kept by Old Joe for safekeeping. They launched the small craft into the water, climbing aboard. The day was warm with fluffy, white clouds floating aimlessly through the bright, blue sky. A pair of mallard ducks flew over the canoe, landing in the water fifty feet from the craft. Grey Wolf and Rose loved to watch wildlife and interact with nature; a large variety of birds called this lake home. In the spring and summer, the water is alive with family life. Mating pairs of waterfowl hatch out large broods of chicks, who swim with their parents on the lake, always looking for food to fill their hungry bellies. Eagles and hawks nest in the trees which border the water, an abundant supply of fish, small mammals, and young birds keeping these avian predators from going hungry.

The couple paddled the shoreline, observing nature at its best. A bull moose, with a large rack of antlers, hardly gave the couple a notice. The moose stood in the tall grass along the shoreline, eating and minding his own business. Grey Wolf and Rose paddled their canoe quietly past this majestic animal, known as the king of the north woods. The canoe glided over the calm water with ease, requiring little effort to paddle. They steered the canoe out into the middle of the lake, where the lake trout lived, preferring deep water with a rocky bottom. Along with whitefish, these two species dominated the fish population in this lake.

Grey Wolf found an area which looked good for fishing. Rose readied the fishnet, hoping to catch the trout coming off the lake bottom, as they moved closer to the surface looking for food. Grey Wolf steadied the canoe with his paddle while Rose threw the fishnet into the water. After waiting a short time, Rose pulled in the net, revealing two lake trout and three whitefish. One more cast of the net caught more trout and two whitefish. The couple were happy with the results of their trip and decided to go back to their cabin, where a nervous Charlie was waiting. Dogs, living as pets in the bush, did not like being left alone without their owners present.

Grey Wolf and Rose left for home. Upon nearing their cabin, the couple heard a loud splash along the shoreline. The forest grew quiet, as a beaver used his tail to warn of impending danger. The animal was alerting all wildlife in the vicinity to be aware of a possible threat from a predator called man. The couple landed the canoe and pulled the craft onshore. Grey Wolf and Rose took the fish to the shed to be cleaned later. Grey Wolf was planning on smoking the fish, increasing the longevity of the meat being edible.

After securing the fish in the shed, the couple returned to their cabin and a waiting Charlie, who had not slept a wink since they left. Grey Wolf fed the young husky whitefish, the dog's favorite meal. Grey Wolf and Rose ate some jerky they had purchased in Dawson, saving room for the big meal the couple were going to enjoy tonight. Having smoked lake trout for dinner was a hungry settler's dream, a wish this young couple would be enjoying shortly.

CHAPTER FOUR

Rose carried more wood to the smoker, where she had started a fire earlier. Grey Wolf was busy in the fur shed, cleaning the fish and getting it ready to cook. A wayward fox had caught the scent of the fish being cleaned. As the animal approached the fur shed, Charlie, who was with Grey Wolf, sensed the fox's presence, quickly turning on the smaller animal and chasing him off into the forest. Charlie returned to the shed with his tail wagging. Grey Wolf praised his dog and fed him some fish as a reward for his brave behaviour.

The fox would become a return visitor, always looking for a handout, which he would usually get from Grey Wolf. Rose eventually named him Savage, because he was so timid. Savage would become part of the family, burrowing a tunnel under the cabin and taking up residence close to his food source. Savage and Charlie would form a cordial relationship, at the urging of Grey Wolf and Rose.

Grey Wolf placed the fish in the smoker. He gave some fillets he had cut from the trout to Rose to cook on the woodstove for dinner tonight. The smoked fish they would save to eat later. During the evening, the couple sat around the campfire eating their dinner. Grey Wolf was growing concerned about how quickly time was passing, as preparations for the winter would need to be started soon. Wood for the woodstove needed to be cut and stacked by the cabin. The fur shed needed to be repaired, as well as the dog yard and shelters. Additionally, a small barn for livestock needed to be built.

Grey Wolf suggested to Rose they visit his father and ask for a loan to pay for the supplies required to accomplish everything needing to be done at their cabin. Grey Wolf's father had acquired considerable wealth during his lifetime, selling and trading furs and raisings dogs needed for transportation during the winter in the Dawson City area. Grey Wolf would offer to repay his father over time, believing the loan would not be an issue, as his father would go along with the plan knowing the money was going to help his son and Rose, who was like a daughter to him.

The couple decided to leave in the morning, taking Charlie with them in the canoe. They would make a stop at Steward's cabin, asking him to watch Charlie, before continuing to Grey Wolf's father's camp in the forest. Grey Wolf also wanted to talk to Steward about a friend of his who had a sawmill a short distance from Steward's cabin. Grey Wolf needed lumber to build the livestock barn and repair his fur shed and dog houses. He hoped if he gave Steward the measurements for the required wood, Steward would order the lumber and arrange delivery to Grey Wolf's cabin.

Grey Wolf told Rose he hoped Steward would be agreeable to this plan, and open his arms wide to help them maneuver the hard road through the first winter in their new home.

CHAPTER FIVE

Grey Wolf and Rose were up at sunrise. They packed some of the lake trout Joe had smoked last night, which they would share with Steward and Blossom when they reached their cabin. Grey Wolf secured the cabin door with extra wood, making it difficult for unwanted intruders to break into the structure while looking for food. A breach of these defences, with an animal entering the cabin, could leave a mess which would take considerable time to clean up. The couple, with Charlie in tow, walked to the lake. Grey Wolf and Rose retrieved the canoe from its resting place and launched the boat into the lake. All the party, including Charlie, took their respective seats in the canoe.

Charlie's excellent behaviour in the boat was the result of training he had received from Steward. Charlie was the dog Steward had chosen for companionship. Charlie and Steward had became close, which led him to take Charlie out in the canoe with him on numerous occasions. Since the previous loss of two beloved pets, Steward had refrained from getting too close to his dogs. This was why he gifted Charlie to Grey Wolf and Rose, he didn't want to continue being close to the dog and be heartbroken if something happened to him. Steward knew they would provide a loving and safe home for Charlie.

The couple had to paddle the canoe across an expanse of open water to reach a channel which connected their lake to the body of water Steward's cabin sat on. Many men and women have lost their lives when sudden storms come up, creating large waves which can flip canoes. These hapless souls are left to the mercy of nature, drowning in the cold water of the lake.

The trio made it safely across the lake and soon found themselves in the channel which separated the two bodies of water. Another hour in the canoe, found them looking at Steward and Blossom's cabin on the opposite shore. The couple were not expecting company; Grey Wolf and Rose's visit would be a surprise. They beached the canoe on Steward's property, disembarked from the craft, and walked towards Steward's cabin. The huskies howled out a warning to their owner in unison, indicating strangers were on his property. Steward, alerted by the dogs' barking, opened the cabin door to greet their company.

Charlie bounded into the structure, overjoyed at seeing Steward and Blossom. Grey Wolf and Rose were introduced to Blossom and invited inside for a cup of coffee. Grey Wolf told Steward of his plans and asked Steward and Blossom if they would help the young couple. Steward and Blossom agreed to let the dog stay with them, as they would enjoy Charlie's company again for a couple of days. Steward extended a hand of friendship, asking them to stay for dinner and spend the night. Grey Wolf readily accepted this generous offer, planning to leave tomorrow morning for his father's camp. It was a day Grey Wolf and Rose were looking forward to.

CHAPTER SIX

The morning dawned early for Grey Wolf and Rose. The two couples had enjoyed eating dinner outside around the campfire the evening before. The night was warm, so the visiting couple decided to sleep outside by the fire. Charlie spent the night inside the cabin with Steward and Blossom. Upon opening their eyes in the morning, the pleasant melody of bird song greeted Rose and Grey Wolf. Steward was awake, letting Charlie outside the cabin to go to the bathroom. The dog ran over and snuggled with Grey Wolf and Rose, letting them know he loved them and had not forgotten about them, even though he had spent the night with Steward and Blossom. The couple returned the love to Charlie, who after this interaction went happily on his way.

Grey Wolf and Rose got up from the hard ground. They ate some jerky they had carried with them for breakfast. They said goodbye to Steward and Blossom, thanking them for their hospitality and good company while they were visiting. The couple and Charlie accompanied Grey Wolf and Rose to their canoe, wishing them a safe journey and telling them they would see them on their return trip home.

Grey Wolf and Rose waved goodbye and soon were out of sight of the couple and their dog.

Grey Wolf's father was at a hunting camp set up during the summer months to provide food for the tribe. The location of his father's camp in the forest was two lakes away from Steward's cabin and would take three hours to reach by canoe. The trip was uneventful until almost reaching their destination, when Grey Wolf's canoe started taking on water. Sitting on shore and not being used since last fall had allowed the seams of the canoe to dry out, causing the craft to leak. Luck had followed the couple on this trip, as their canoe started leaking just as the tribe's canoes, which were sitting on the shoreline, came into view.

Grey Wolf and Rose steered their boat onto the sandy shore where the other canoes lay. Relieved to have made it safely to shore, Grey Wolf would employ the services of his father to reseal the seams in the old birch bark canoe. A well-worn path into the bush led Grey Wolf and Rose to the Indigenous hunting camp set up in the forest. Grey Wolf's father oversaw this camp, its purpose being to provide fresh meat to the tribal members who were not self sustaining because of age or health. The camp was busy, as women and children stayed here with their men who were part of the hunting parties. Grey Wolf's father was in camp when the young couple arrived.

Grey Wolf's father, Blazing Eagle, was a well-respected member of the tribe and next in line for the title of Chief. He welcomed his son and Rose into camp, surprised, but pleased, to see them there. Blazing Eagle called for a celebration to mark the visit of his son and daughter-in-law.

A meal would be prepared, and the party which followed would include drumming, dancing, and singing.

Blazing Eagle went to look at Grey Wolf's canoe and after inspecting it, told his son to pull it away from the other boats it sat with. Blazing Eagle left the area, returning a short time later with the tree gum needed to seal the leaks in the boat. With Grey Wolf's help, Blazing Eagle completed the repairs, saying the canoe would be ready for use by morning.

After their lengthy paddle, the couple accepted Blazing Eagle's offer of a tent they could use to nap and freshen up before the night's festivities. It was a welcomed gesture the tired and excited Grey Wolf and Rose would not turn down, as they were looking forward to enjoying the night's celebration.

CHAPTER SEVEN

Blazing Eagle had instructed two men in camp to erect a shelter for his son, Grey Wolf, and his daughter-in-law, Rose, to use while they were visiting. After the repairs to Grey Wolf's canoe were finished, the trio returned to the camp. The men were finishing the work on the tepee, allowing the couple to take a nap before dinner. Grey Wolf and Rose fell into a peaceful sleep, not waking until Blazing Eagle woke them. The couple woke up in time to prepare for dinner and the pow wow afterward.

The odour of deer meat cooking on campfires filled the air with tantalizing smells and a promise of a delicious dinner. A young buck, which had been shot the day before, provided venison as the main course for the evening meal. Produce, grown in the tribal garden which had been planted in a clearing near the camp, and fish, caught from the lake, would supplement the venison.

Grey Wolf and Rose arrived at the festivities, seating themselves with Blazing Eagle. Mounds of meat and vegetables were waiting to be eaten. After the eating and socializing were over, the second half of the party was about to begin. The sound of drumbeats filled the forest. Dancers, dressed in traditional clothing, danced in a circle, chanting and shaking rattles made from gourds grown in the gardens. The party went on until midnight, the campfires allowed to burn down to embers as the tired partiers found sleep in their shelters.

During the evening, Grey Wolf had talked to his father about the loan he needed to do repairs at his newly acquired cabin. He told his father how they had come into possession of Old Joe's cabin and the surprisingly good condition it was in. Grey Wolf told his father, with a few upgrades it would be a comfortable home for himself and Rose. Blazing Eagle was happy to give the young couple the loan, providing his son with a sizable amount of gold. With a wink to Grey Wolf, he said the gold should make the loan total about a hundred dollars. Grey Wolf and Rose thanked Blazing Eagle for his generosity.

The couple retired for the evening, planning to return to Steward's cabin and their waiting dog, Charlie, in the morning. The dawn sky beckoned a clear day, as Grey Wolf and Rose left camp in their repaired canoe. The couple realized how fortunate they were the canoe hadn't started leaking when they were in the middle of one of the lakes on their journey here. An unfortunate accident like that would have left the couple in the cold water, most likely causing them to perish. That was a fate the couple hoped they could avoid, in this land which gave only one reward, survival.

CHAPTER EIGHT

As Grey Wolf and Rose paddled their canoe, the water on lake was calm and the day was sunny and warm. The couple's thoughts were silent, as an uncertain future unfolded in front of them. Grey Wolf wondered if he had made the right decision, removing himself and Rose from the security of living in a native village with other tribe members, for a life in a forest cabin alone.

After a serene trip across two lakes, the couple found themselves within view of Steward's cabin. Shortly after this observation, Grey Wolf and Rose were beaching the canoe on the shoreline. Charlie was the first one to notice the couple had arrived back from their journey visiting Grey Wolf's father. Upon seeing Grey Wolf and Rose, the dog bounded happily toward them. The couple returned the greeting, hugging Charlie tightly. The trio walked toward the cabin, yelling out a greeting to Steward and Blossom.

Steward came to his door, glad to see Grey Wolf and Rose had safely made it back. He invited the couple inside for coffee. Charlie chose to stay outside, as he had been busy chasing squirrels when Grey Wolf and Rose had arrived. Charlie wanted to return to what he had been doing.

Over coffee, Grey Wolf told Steward about their canoe leaking. Steward replied he had a friend die in the middle of a lake under similar circumstances. Having a leak develop when far from shore, is not what anyone would wish for while canoeing. Steward told Grey Wolf he had visited his friend with the sawmill and gave the man the measurements Grey Wolf had provided. The lumber would be ready in ten days and would be delivered by boat to Grey Wolf and Rose's cabin. Grey Wolf thanked Steward, telling him he needed to travel to Dawson to cash in some gold his father had given him in order to make payment.

It was decided Grey Wolf and Rose would spend the night with Steward and Blossom before leaving for home in the morning. Steward invited the couple for dinner, telling them he had shot and smoked grouse yesterday afternoon. He had also shot a rabbit in his front yard this morning, before Grey Wolf and Rose arrived. This food meant an enjoyable dinner around the campfire this evening for the two couples.

Blossom started the campfire early, for Steward to cook the rabbit over. A raven, noticing the smoke from the campfire, was waiting high in a tree above the cabin for an opportunity to feed off the scraps of these hungry humans. The couples sat around the fire, with darkness settling over them. Stars lit up the cloudless sky and peace washed over these couples, who had handed their lives over to nature for a chance at survival which they felt they deserved.

CHAPTER NINE

Charlie was the first to wake in the cabin the following morning. He approached Grey Wolf and Rose, who were sleeping on the floor. Charlie bent down and gave Grey Wolf a slobbery kiss, causing him to open his eyes, only to see Charlie staring into his face. He pulled himself off the floor and opened the cabin door for the waiting dog to be let outside. The rest of the occupants of the cabin were soon awake, joining Grey Wolf for coffee.

Steward and Blossom could offer no breakfast to their company, as they had eaten everything last night. After Grey Wolf and Rose finished their coffee, they packed their few belongings to leave. They thanked Steward and Blossom for their help and hospitality, leaving the couple waving from the shore, as they left in the canoe with Charlie.

The placid waters of the lake mesmerized Grey Wolf and Rose as they earnestly paddled the craft homeward. Charlie sat up in the front of the canoe watching, as if guiding the way home. A sudden honking caught Grey Wolf's attention. A flock of Canadian geese were flying low in their direction. Grey Wolf grabbed his rifle, expecting to take advantage of this situation. The geese, ignoring the canoe and its occupants, flew over the heads of the couple and Charlie. Two rounds from Grey Wolf's gun left two birds laying lifeless, close by in the water. Rose steered the canoe over to where the geese lay floating and Grey Wolf reached over the side of the canoe, pulling them from the water. When they arrived at their cabin, he would clean and dress the birds for smoking.

Summers in the Yukon were spent in a constant search for food. No refrigeration meant food harvested needed to be eaten the same day or the next. Food poisoning was something to avoid at all cost. More than a few starving men have died from eating rancid meat; dying from starvation or poisoning was not a pleasant ordeal while alone in the bush.

Charlie sounded the alarm, barking with tail wagging when he spotted the familiar sight of home. A short time later, the couple were beaching the canoe in front of their cabin. Charlie was the first out of the boat, making a long jump onto the shore. He ran to the cabin, nose buried in the grass, smelling for new or unusual odours. When Charlie reached the front door of the cabin, he barked when he noticed something was different.

Grey Wolf and Rose exited the canoe, pulling the craft up on the shore. They walked to the cabin to see why Charlie was barking. Grey Wolf noticed they had had a visitor while they were gone. Some of the extra boards Grey Wolf had placed across the cabin door were lying on the ground. Large scratch marks were visible on the cabin door, indicating a bear had tried to make entry into the cabin. It appeared it had failed to breach Grey Wolf's added security. This was a lucky break for the travellers, who had just arrived home, and a lost opportunity for the hungry bear.

CHAPTER TEN

Grey Wolf finished removing the extra wood he had used to secure the cabin door, allowing Rose and Charlie to enter the structure. Grey Wolf walked back to the lake to retrieve the two geese from the floor of the canoe. Grabbing the birds by the neck, Grey Wolf carried the geese to the shed where he would prepare the birds to be smoked. He entered the cabin, asking Rose if she would start a fire in the smoker for him. She told him she would do it as soon as she finished starting the fire in the woodstove. Rose needed to boil water for Grey Wolf to submerge the geese in, which would allow for the easier removal of the geese's feathers.

Grey Wolf surmised he would rather butcher a deer than clean a goose. However, he knew the results of his labor today would be delicious smoked goose for dinner. After the tedious job of pulling feathers from the birds' bodies, he cut the geese into smaller pieces and placed the meat in the smoker. Grey Wolf would leave the goose there all day and the couple and Charlie would eat the cooked meat for dinner tonight.

The evening soon set upon Grey Wolf and Rose's cabin. Grey Wolf removed the goose from the smoker and the couple sat around a campfire Grey Wolf had started for ambience. They shared the delicious goose, which nature had provided, giving a healthy portion to Charlie who sat at their feet. A raven sat high in a nearby treetop, watching and waiting for the couple to return to their cabin for the night. Then, the bird would swoop down to the ground, looking for scraps left over from dinner.

Grey Wolf and Rose discussed going to Dawson tomorrow to cash in their gold. Grey Wolf needed money to pay for the lumber being delivered from the sawmill to his cabin. While in Dawson, the couple would stay at Bev's house for the night, hopeful she would also welcome Charlie. The quiet emanating from the forest, and staring at the glowing embers of the campfire, caused the couple to become drowsy, sending them indoors to bed. The raven swooped down from his perch high above the cabin, foraging for scraps of meat which had fallen on the ground while the couple were eating. The raven found enough food to make his wait worthwhile.

The bright rays of the rising sun shone into the cabin through the windows. Grey Wolf opened his eyes, seeing dawn was waning. He woke Mary, telling her he wanted to get started for Dawson soon. Mary pulled herself out of bed and started preparations to leave. She gathered up the few belongings they would need, and then Grey Wolf boarded up the cabin, calling Charlie, who was out of sight. They left the cabin for the four hour walk to Dawson.

Grey Wolf hoped to shoot some grouse on their way to Dawson to provide fresh meat for Bev to cook for dinner. After a two hour walk, the trio stopped to rest beside a small lake full of game birds. With little effort, Grey Wolf shot three ducks, which would provide plenty of meat for these hungry travellers and their host tonight. The group continued on their way, reaching Bev's house with no further disruptions.

Charlie arrived at Bev's front door first, his barking drawing the attention of the people in the house. Bev opened her door, giving Grey Wolf and Rose each a hug. She reached down and patted Charlie's head, telling him he was welcome too. An added surprise was that Jason, Wendy, and their son were in Dawson. They had returned Omar, their donkey, to Bev's barn, after using him for work at their cabin. The couple would also be staying at Bev's house overnight, returning to their home in the morning.

Hospitality can never be forgotten when the odds are stacked against you. Bev was a saviour in the forest, a title this busy woman deserved.

CHAPTER ELEVEN

Jason offered to help Grey Wolf clean the ducks, which Bev greatly appreciated. When finished with this chore, Grey Wolf and Rose decided to visit the gold dealer in town to cash in the gold Grey Wolf's father had given them. The couple left their dog with Bev, allowing Jason and Wendy's son, Kuzih, to play with him. Charlie let Kuzih climb on him, showing no displeasure. When Kuzih stopped playing, Charlie would whine or bark, inviting the boy to continue.

Jason and Wendy took Kuzih out to Bev's barn to visit the donkeys. The young boy especially liked Baby Jack, who would be turning a year old in September. When the trio entered the barn, a mouse appeared out of the nearby hay pile, running across Wendy's feet, scaring her half to death. As usual, the donkeys were glad to see anyone come in the barn, braying in harmony at the family's arrival. Pigeons cooed in the rafters, a nest of their babies in full view for the visitors to see. After visiting with the donkeys, the couple decided to walk through the barn. Finding nothing interesting, they went outside to the chicken coup, where Jason and Wendy let Kuzih collect any eggs the hens had laid for Bev. After finding three eggs, the couple and their son returned to Bev's house.

Grey Wolf and Rose walked into the gold dealer's business. After weighing their precious metal, the man offered Grey Wolf two hundred dollars. Grey Wolf now understood why his father had winked at him when he told him the gold was worth a hundred dollars. The couple left, surprised and happy with the amount of cash they now had. On their way back to Bev's house, they stopped to purchase coffee and sugar, at an inflated price. Commodities such as these were rare and costly in Dawson.

Upon returning to Bev's house, the couple found Charlie asleep by the woodstove. Wendy told Rose her son had tired Charlie out with his rambunctious play. Bev was busy in the kitchen cooking dinner. She was roasting the ducks, which would be accompanied with vegetables from her garden. Her fresh baked bread and berry pie topped off the menu.

The calendar had turned from July to August, ushering in a month of subtle change; a transition from the warm summer months to the cooler days of fall was approaching. Bev's meal was delicious, as usual, and the company at dinner was great. Dinner was followed by dessert and coffee in Bev's living room. Shortly afterwards, the talk turned to yawns, prompting Bev and the young couples to call it a night. Tomorrow would come early, and the walk home would be long. A peaceful sleep is what the two couples longed for.

CHAPTER TWELVE

The smell of Bev cooking breakfast downstairs was the first thing to greet Grey Wolf's senses when he woke from his night's sleep. The first rays of the rising sun shone through the couple's window, illuminating the room. Grey Wolf shook Rose, telling her to wake up. He told her Bev was going to be calling them down to the kitchen for breakfast shortly.

Jason, Wendy, and their son, Kuzih, were also awake. They walked by Grey Wolf and Rose's bedroom door on their way downstairs to the kitchen, just as Grey Wolf and Rose were getting ready to exit their door. The group chuckled at the coincidence, wishing each other a good morning. When everyone was seated around the table, Bev served the food. This would be the last delicious breakfast the young couples would enjoy until they stayed overnight here again.

Bev had access to food which could not be found when living in the forests of the Yukon. The fur trappers and gold prospectors who called this place home lived on a diet which was heavy on meat, supplemented with edible plants gathered from the forest when they were in season.

After the group of family and friends finished breakfast, the two couples packed their belongings and hugged Bev goodbye. The day was sunny and warm, with only wispy, white clouds floating across the blue sky. The music of bird song filled the forest with pleasant melodies. The two families and their dogs walked together for a short distance, before heading off on their separate ways.

Grey Wolf and Rose trekked on, with Charlie leading the way. The couple soon reached the halfway point on their walk home, where they decided to take a break and stop for a rest. They stopped at an outcropping, which overlooked a beautiful lake. The placid, blue waters shone like a diamond in the bright sunshine. A tree covered island in the middle of the lake, surrounded by rocky shores, was awe-inspiring to the young couple, a true gift from nature, which could not be replicated.

After resting for thirty minutes, the couple and Charlie continued their journey home. Two hours passed before Grey Wolf's cabin came into view. The structure looked the same way as when they had left. After entering the cabin, Grey Wolf suggested to Rose they should take the canoe out on the lake to fish or hunt waterfowl for food. The couple had nothing to eat, a common problem during the summer months due to the lack of refrigeration.

Rose started a fire in the woodstove to take the dampness out of the cabin. Charlie was already laying in his favorite spot, on the floor beside the stove. Grey Wolf and Rose let Charlie be when they left the cabin to go to the lake. They retrieved the canoe from under the evergreen and launched the boat into the water. The couple paddled to the area where they knew the trout congregated in large numbers.

Rose laid the fishnet into the calm water of the lake. After letting the net float underwater with the current while Grey Wolf paddled, Rose was ready to pull the net back into the canoe. Her prize was enough fish for dinner, with two whitefish included for Charlie. Not wanting to take more fish than what they could use, the couple returned to their cabin and their waiting dog. Dinner tonight was now a sure thing, a nice outcome for a hungry couple living in the wilderness, where securing food was not always a given.

CHAPTER THIRTEEN

Upon returning to the cabin from fishing, Grey Wolf started a fire in the smoker. After cleaning the trout, he placed the fillets in the smoker, hoping they would be ready to eat for dinner. He then returned to the inside of the cabin to see what Rose was doing.

He found his wife engrossed in a book she had found at Bev's house. She had borrowed the book, telling Bev she would return it on their next trip to Dawson. Rose had been schooled in English when she lived with Grey Wolf's parents, who could both speak and read the language. Grey Wolf had been responsible for teaching Rose to read and write English. The couple still spoke their native language, conversing in both languages equally to one another.

Mid-afternoon, Rose walked outside to the smoker to check on the fish which was cooking. She was happy to report to Grey Wolf they would be eating succulent lake trout for dinner. A cool August breeze blew in through the open cabin windows. The smell of the forest filled the home with the aroma of nature, soothing the turbulent spirits of this wilderness couple.

The distant sound of thunder could be heard, growing fainter as time passed by. The quiet atmosphere in the cabin caused Grey Wolf to fall asleep sitting up in his chair while at the kitchen table. He was abruptly woken by the sound of Charlie barking. Getting up to investigate, he heard voices outside. It was Steward, who had arrived at the couple's cabin by canoe.

Steward had come to inform Grey Wolf his order of lumber from the sawmill was ready earlier than expected and would be delivered tomorrow. The owner of the sawmill had constructed a large, flat-bottomed boat to transport logs and lumber across the lakes to wilderness cabins. Finished lumber was sold to anyone fortunate enough to have money to spend. The wood was used to keep their cabins and outbuildings in good condition.

Steward spent two hours visiting with Grey Wolf and Rose before leaving their cabin, wanting to get home to Blossom before darkness set in. Grey Wolf started a campfire, keeping a low flame on the wood. The couple would eat the fish while enjoying the ambience of the fire later this evening. He returned to the cabin, where the couple relaxed while the fish finished smoking. Using a small fire in the smoker allowed the fish to cook slowly, which Grey Wolf felt made the fish juicier and more succulent.

The sun was sinking low in the evening sky when Grey Wolf, Rose, and Charlie sat around the campfire to eat the fish. The sky was clear of cloud cover and a million pins of light shone in the settling darkness of the night sky.

The trout was steaming hot and fell apart when Grey Wolf removed it from the smoker. After letting the fish cool, the family ate this delicious meal together, until there was nothing left to eat, not even scraps for the raven. Grey Wolf and Rose thought it was a wonderful way to end the day in the Yukon.

CHAPTER FOURTEEN

The howls of a wolf pack woke Grey Wolf and Rose from what had been an undisturbed slumber. A recent uptick in the number of wolves howling at night suggested a pack of the animals had moved into this area. The predators were claiming this land as their new hunting ground. Charlie was also listening to the wolves, knowing he now had to be aware of enemies which had moved into his territory. The wolf pack would soon make a visit to Grey Wolf and Rose's to investigate this anomaly in the forest. The animals would come periodically at night, looking for meat which had mistakenly been left out, unsecured by the cabin owners.

Grey Wolf and Rose quickly fell back asleep, not waking until the early hours of the morning. Steward had told Grey Wolf to expect Tim, the owner of the sawmill, to arrive with his lumber order before noon. A sudden barking from Charlie and the sound of an animal's hoofbeats drew the attention of Grey Wolf. A glance out the open cabin door caught Charlie chasing a deer across the front yard. Grey Wolf laughed when he thought of Charlie running any more than a hundred yards chasing this deer. Grey Wolf was expecting his dog to return home shortly, out of breath and looking for water.

The morning passed by with no sign of Tim and his lumber. Grey Wolf waited patiently for the man to arrive. His wishes were answered a little after noon, when he saw Tim's boat approaching his cabin. After docking the boat, introductions were made followed by handshakes. With everyone working, including Rose and Tim's helper, the lumber was unloaded quickly and stacked near the cabin. Tim told Grey Wolf he also cut and sold firewood, which he delivered in pieces needing to be split with an axe. He informed Grey Wolf he had a pile of wood at his sawmill which was dry and ready to burn.

Grey Wolf, who was already worried about cutting enough wood, negotiated a deal with Tim to buy enough firewood for the winter. Tim would deliver this valuable commodity to Grey Wolf's cabin in early October. The men shook hands to cement the deal, with Grey Wolf then going to his cabin to retrieve the cash to pay for the lumber and delivery charge. He also gave Tim a deposit on the firewood, which he promised to bring. Tim and his helper left for home on the empty craft, which, being lighter in weight, promised an easier time navigating home.

Grey Wolf and Rose walked to where they had piled the lumber and found the wood to be of high quality; the cut from the saw was sharp and the measurements precise. The priority for the lumber was using the wood to rebuild the fur shed. Grey Wolf had determined the current structure had too much rotten lumber to merely repair it. Eventually, he would need to go back to Dawson and buy a small woodstove to replace the one currently in the old building. He knew the current woodstove and pipes were a fire hazard; an accident waiting to happen. Safety was a top priority when living in the bush, as loss of property sometimes meant a loss of life in this frozen and inhospitable land. One chance is given to man by nature, and his personal decisions can determine whether he lives or dies.

CHAPTER FIFTEEN

The waning days of August brought cooler temperatures and shorter days to the far north. The waterfowl living on these wilderness lakes in the Yukon would be leaving soon, their habitat becoming frozen in ice. Nearing the end of September, the bird activity will increase, with flocks of geese and other waterfowl using the lake which fronted Grey Wolf and Rose's cabin as a stopping point on their long migration south. Before the bird migrations end in late October, Grey Wolf will hunt and shoot many ducks and some geese. The cooler weather, and the use of their outdoor freezer, will help keep the meat from the birds fresh for a longer period than during the summer, making their quest for food not as pressing.

On a warm day shortly after the lumber was delivered from the sawmill, Grey Wolf and Rose received a surprise visit from Joe, Mary, and their dog, Rusty. They had left their place this morning on a whim and walked the two hours to Grey Wolf and Rose's cabin. The couple were welcomed into the comfortable home Grey Wolf and Rose had made for themselves in the forest.

Rose boiled water on the stove and served coffee to her guests and husband, who were sitting around the kitchen table. The couples discussed the upcoming winter season and fur trapping, giving advice to one another on ways to increase their chances of catching valuable fur.

Grey Wolf turned the conversation to the lumber sitting outside his cabin. He told Joe of his plans to rebuild his fur shed, which needed to be accomplished before the trapping season began. Joe offered to help Grey Wolf with this job, as he was experienced in carpentry and Grey Wolf had everything needed, having purchased a new saw and nails on his last trip to Dawson. Joe told Grey Wolf if they put in long hours, they should be able to complete the work within the next two days.

Joe and Mary decided to spend the night with Grey Wolf and Rose, with the men beginning the carpentry work on the fur shed first thing in the morning. Grey Wolf thought this was a great idea, however, Rose realized there was no food in the cabin and the couples would go hungry tonight. Mary said that was fine, and she and Rose could take the canoe out on the lake while the men worked tomorrow. They should be able to catch enough fish to feed everyone.

The friends enjoyed socializing, a rare commodity when living in the bush. They played the popular card game, euchre, until after midnight. A full moon lit up the night sky, as the last solitary call of the loon came from the lake. These animals' cries would soon be forgotten, as the cold and snow ambushed the land. Rusty and Charlie, always friends, were sharing a space by the woodstove. A feeling of comradeship swept through the cabin, affecting both men and dogs. The loneliness experienced daily by those who called the bush home had temporarily disappeared in this land called the Yukon.

CHAPTER SIXTEEN

The two couples sleeping in the cabin were awakened by a bark from Rusty. The dogs wanted outside, so Grey Wolf pulled himself out of bed to open the cabin door to let both Rusty and Charlie out. He stoked the fire in the woodstove and added more wood to its belly. He put a kettle of water on the stove to boil for coffee. He was hungry and longed for a hearty breakfast, which made his thoughts turn to Bev and the delicious meals she presented to her visiting company.

Joe and Mary rose from their bed on the floor, seating themselves around the kitchen table. Grey Wolf joined them for coffee, after walking over and shaking his wife awake. She rose from the bed and joined everyone at the table. The couples talked about eating breakfast with Bev in Dawson. Laughter spread around the kitchen table at the couples' wishful thinking. After drinking their coffee, the men left the cabin to work on the shed.

The day was sunny and warm, and Grey Wolf was excited about getting this important job finished before the winter season arrived. Rose and Mary would launch the canoe this morning into the lake to try and harvest fish to eat. Eating later today would ward off the hunger the young couples were feeling. The sounds of the saw cutting wood and the hammer hitting nails filled the forest. Rose and Mary launched the canoe to go fishing shortly after the men left the cabin to work on the shed.

The women returned home before lunch, removing the numerous trout and whitefish they had caught from the bottom of the canoe. Rose and Mary cleaned the fish by the lake, planning on frying the fillets for lunch. Rusty and Charlie would be fed the whitefish. Before going in the cabin to prepare the fish, the women walked over to see how their husbands' work was progressing. Rose told the men of their plan to cook and serve fish fillets for lunch. Grey Wolf told his wife to call him and Joe to the cabin when lunch was ready.

While working, Grey Wolf mentioned to Joe that Steward had offered to help with rebuilding the shed. When Joe offered his help, Grey Wolf accepted, as he would rather use Steward's experience helping restructure the yard for his dog team, which was arriving soon. The dog shelters needed to be improved, using salvageable lumber from the fur shed and whatever was left over from the sawmill delivery.

The men continued with their work, until Rose called the men to come in and eat lunch. Upon entering the cabin, the overwhelming smell of cooking fish captured Grey Wolf and Joe's senses. Charlie and Rusty were also waiting patiently for food. The dogs had hunted small rodents, such as mice and squirrels, during this recent food drought, but it was not enough to fill their hungry bellies. All the fish Rose and Mary caught were eaten for lunch.

Another canoe trip was planned for later. This time the women would take rifles, not fishing nets. Rose and Mary hoped to have a surprise for dinner, a meal loved in the Yukon by fur trappers, but not often served in the bush, beaver stew. If they were lucky enough to bag one, they would cook it with fresh vegetables from Rose's garden. It should be a meal to rival one of Bev's, not often served to these ever-hungry homesteaders living in the bush.

CHAPTER SEVENTEEN

Mary and Rose launched the canoe into the calm water of the beautiful northern lake. The first signs of the coming fall were all around them. The vegetation was turning brown, losing its vibrant green colour. The wildflowers were finished blooming, their bright and bold hues would not return until next year. Adult waterfowl were active, no longer under the restraints of raising their young, who would soon be adult birds joining the migration south.

The women paddled the canoe to where the rocky lake bottom gradually turned to soft mud. This area was wetlands, where aquatic mammals lived. Muskrats and beaver called this part of the lake home, and this was where Mary and Rose hoped to shoot a beaver to cook for dinner. The marsh had numerous colonies to choose from, as a healthy supply of beaver lived in this part of the lake.

Old Joe had not trapped any beaver for the two years prior to his passing. As he aged, Old Joe's fingers were crippled from arthritis, making it difficult for him to set the beaver traps and keep the holes cleared of ice. This led the colonies and number of beaver lodges to propagate throughout the wetlands. Mounds of dried grass located above the water line, indicated many muskrats also made this swampy area home.

Rose and Mary quietly paddled the canoe through the wetlands. The atmosphere in the swamp was quiet, except for the bullfrogs croaking their familiar song. As the women approached a lodge, a beaver stuck his head up out of the water, not seeing Rose and Mary sitting in the canoe. Rose, who was holding the rifle waiting for one of these elusive creatures to surface for air, fired off a shot. The sound of the gunshot echoed through the wetlands. The young beaver lay dead, floating in the water, a bullet in the animal's head.

The two women looked at one another with triumphant grins on their faces. They paddled the canoe over to where the dead beaver lay. Rose reached over the side of the boat, pulling the dead animal into the craft. The women left the area, paddling the canoe back to the cabin.

Grey Wolf and Joe were busy working on the shed. One more day of work and they should finish this job. The foundation of the old building was sound, but much of the structure's wood was rotten and had to be replaced. The men salvaged as much of the old lumber from the building as possible; Grey Wolf would burn any unusable wood in a hot campfire some evening.

The sudden appearance by Rose carrying a dead beaver, surprised both Grey Wolf and Joe, who now knew they would be enjoying a good dinner. The women would butcher the beaver, collect vegetables from Rose's garden, and make a delicious stew tonight. This was something the couples would appreciate, sharing the bounty of food nature provided them.

CHAPTER EIGHTEEN

Rose and Mary got to work butchering the beaver Rose had shot earlier in the day. When the beaver was gutted by the women, the overwhelming stench sent Mary into the bush throwing up. Rose, with a stronger stomach, finished cleaning the beaver and taking the smelly innards away from the cabin. Now the women would no longer be disturbed by the foul odor while preparing the beaver meat for the stew.

After working for an hour butchering the mammal, Mary carried the meat from the beaver into the cabin. Rose headed to her vegetable garden to retrieve carrots, a turnip, and some potatoes to cook in the stew. She then walked into the forest to pick some edible mushrooms, which would provide additional flavor. The women worked on preparing the stew while Grey Wolf and Joe continued working on rebuilding the shed.

As Joe was pulling the last rotten section of wood from the building, a small bag fell to the ground, secured closed with a drawstring. Surprised by this sudden discovery, Joe reached down and picked up the leather bag. Loosening the drawstring, he felt inside and pulled out a gold pocket watch. Flipping the cover on the watch open, a small piece of paper revealed it had belonged to Old Joe's grandfather, a family heirloom hidden and forgotten when Old Joe first arrived at this cabin. With the onset of age and senility, the pocket watch's location had been forgotten by Old Joe. Its hiding place in the old shed was never meant to be found.

After finding the watch, the men were ready to call it a day. Grey Wolf noticed smoke billowing from the chimney of his cabin. Like clouds, the dense white smoke drifted into the forest, dissipating among the evergreen trees. Grey Wolf and Joe entered the cabin, where the beaver stew cooking on the woodstove sent a pleasurable aroma throughout the structure. Grey Wolf told the women to stop what they were doing and sit at the kitchen table. He removed the pocket watch from the bag and set it in the center of the table for all to see. Rose and Mary gasped in disbelief when they realized a valuable family heirloom from Old Joe had been found in the dilapidated shed.

Grey Wolf hid the watch in a secure place until it could be sold. He would reward Joe for finding the treasure when the sale of the watch was final, and he had been paid for the transaction. A celebratory atmosphere was enjoyed over the dinner table. The work on the shed would be completed tomorrow and there was enough stew left over for another day. Rusty and Charlie ate dry dog food, which both couples provided their dogs with when no other food was available, with a bit of stew mixed in. This was sufficient to take care of the gnawing hunger the animals' felt in their stomachs.

As the evening progressed, the howling of the wolf pack sent a loud message to the animals living close by. Rusty and Charlie listened to their enemies' song, that of a predator with no empathy for huskies.

CHAPTER NINETEEN

As the morning dawn was announcing another day, the sound of approaching thunder woke the sleeping occupants of the cabin. The dogs, fearful of the thunder, moved to their owners' sides looking for comfort until the storm passed. Heavy rain pounded on the cabin roof, while bright flashes of lightning lit up the early morning sky. A leak in the roof allowed rainwater into the cabin, dripping from the ceiling onto the kitchen table. The building leaked only when flooding rain fell. Grey Wolf would put the leak on his list of jobs which needed to be done around the cabin.

The rain passed quickly, with bright sunshine following closely behind the storm. Rose, being the first one up, let the waiting Charlie and Rusty outside. She stoked the embers in the woodstove and added more wood to the fire, placing a kettle of water on the cooktop to boil. She planned to brew coffee as soon as the water was hot.

The bright sun was quickly drying the land. Grey Wolf and Joe, after spending thirty minutes conversing with their wives around the kitchen table, left the cabin to continue working on the shed. Rose and Mary planned to collect berries from the forest today. After eating the rest of the stew for dinner, they would enjoy this treat for dessert.

Grey Wolf and Joe returned to their work site. By the early afternoon they had completed the job, a sturdy shed standing where the old one once stood. A positive outcome such as this was not always the case, as many different factors can arise causing construction projects to not get finished. The number one reason why this happens is running out of building materials. Grey Wolf had planned well, having enough lumber left over from his order to work with Steward on repairing the dog shelters. He had changed his mind about building a livestock barn, due to the dangers from bears and wolves who owned this territory.

The women had returned from berry picking, which had been a successful venture. A large bucket of black raspberries sat on the kitchen table, ready to eat. Mary sprinkled a little sugar over the berries before serving them to her company. The group ended their evening sitting around the campfire, eating the sweet treat the women had collected.

The evening was warm, under a clear sky filled with twinkling stars. The campfire crackled, sending smoke up into the still night air. Savage, the fox, watched from the shadows, his presence unknown to the couples sitting around the campfire. He was looking for something to eat, but wary of approaching the strangers who accompanied Grey Wolf and Rose. Searching for food was a common denominator between man and animal in this savage land, where sustenance was earned and not a given.

CHAPTER TWENTY

Their visit having gone well, with even Rusty and Charlie having a good time, Joe and Mary left Grey Wolf and Rose's cabin early in the morning for the two hour walk home. Grey Wolf promised a reciprocal visit from himself and Rose before Christmas. Joe and Mary turned and waved goodbye as they disappeared around a bend in the trail. Grey Wolf and Rose, with Charlie in tow, retreated into their now quiet cabin.

The life of a fur trapper was not easy. In the winter, he was forced to check his trapline daily because of predators and scavengers, who would steal and eat dead mammals found in his traps. This caused the fur to be ruined, making the hides unsalable. After blizzards, the hapless men and women who chose this way of life, were forced to dig their traps out from under feet of snow. A few of their traps would be impossible to find, not recovered until the snow melted in the spring. Survival in the wilderness of Canada's far north was a challenge; starvation, cabin fever, and freezing, taking the lives of many of these early adventurers who tested their luck.

Grey Wolf and Rose had accepted the challenge when

they left the security of their tribe and moved into the forest together. The couple had married, choosing life in a cabin, alone in the wilderness as man and wife. The Indigenous couple loved the interactions with nature they faced daily. Having been raised in the forest and learning the ways of survival from Grey Wolf's father, an experienced hunter and gatherer, would prove to be an enormous asset. He had taught Grey Wolf and Rose how to build emergency shelters in time of need and where to find food when no other source could be found.

Grey Wolf and Rose decided to take Charlie and go on a trip. They would travel by canoe to Steward and Blossom's cabin and spend the night. The following day, the couple would walk two hours to Johnathan and Shining Star's cabin, to finally meet Rose's cousin and her family. Bev had informed Rose of all the relatives living in the bush, and Shining Star was the one cousin she had yet to meet.

The following morning, Charlie sensed Grey Wolf and Rose were getting ready to go somewhere and was excited and ready to leave. Grey Wolf secured the cabin door and the couple left, walking to the lake. They retrieved the birch bark canoe from under the evergreen, pushing the craft onto the pristine, blue waters. Charlie took his seat in the front of the boat, while Grey Wolf and Rose took their familiar seats in the canoe. They pushed off from shore, paddling the canoe out onto the water.

With good weather, the trip across the two lakes to Steward and Bossom's cabin took two hours. The journey was uneventful and soon the couple heard a recognition bark from Charlie, letting them know they were getting close to their destination, as Steward's cabin came into view on the distant shoreline. A large amount of smoke could be seen rising from outside the cabin. Rose suggested to Grey Wolf, Steward was using his smoker to cook fish or meat. Steward always seemed to have smoked fish on hand when visiting his cabin.

The trio had made it safely to their destination, looking forward to seeing Steward and Blossom's happy faces when they opened their cabin door. Friendships in the Yukon were treasured by the few residents who enjoyed them, human contact a must in this land of isolation and despair.

CHAPTER TWENTY-ONE

Steward's huskies barked loudly, letting Steward and Blossom know someone was on their property. Steward got up from the kitchen table and looked out the window. He told Blossom he saw Grey Wolf, Rose, and Charlie walking towards their cabin from the lake. Steward opened the door to greet his friends, inviting them into the cabin for coffee.

Blossom greeted Grey Wolf and Rose with a hug. Grey Wolf told Steward about their plans for a meet and greet with Johnathan and Shining Star. Steward told the couple Johnathan and Shining Star were looking forward to meeting them. The couple had visited Steward and Blossom a short time ago and the topic of Grey Wolf and Rose had come up during their conversation. Steward had shared how much he liked the couple and Shining Star had expressed she was anxious to meet them. Johnathan had informed Blossom and Steward to please let Grey Wolf and Rose know they were welcome to come visit them anytime.

Grey Wolf told Steward he had completed the work on the fur shed with Joe's help, and there was enough lumber to refurbish the dog houses, but not enough to build anything else. Steward told Grey Wolf he would come by his cabin in a couple of weeks to help him get the dog yard ready for his new team. He also invited the couple to stay overnight, saying he had plenty of smoked fish for everyone to eat tonight sitting around the campfire. Grey Wolf laughed, repeating what Rose had said to him about there always being smoked fish available at Steward's home.

The two couples and Charlie enjoyed the afternoon together. Steward and Blossom had been working on clearing a walking path around the lake their cabin sat on and invited Grey Wolf and Rose to join them on the part of the trail they had already cleared. A few wildflowers, which were late in their bloom, were scattered along the shore of the lake. Small groups of ducks congregated along the shoreline, looking for food in the shallow water. A sudden gust of wind blew a few leaves off the deciduous trees, as the couples walked along the trail. Their leaves would soon be changing from their summer foliage, to sending a bounty of colours to the forest floor.

After a thirty-minute walk, they reached the end of the path which had been cleared. The group turned around, walking back to Steward's cabin. Mary told Blossom she loved the new trail Steward and she were clearing, and she and Grey Wolf would like to traverse the circumference of the lake once the trail was finished. Steward told Grey Wolf he and Blossom were planning on selecting a beautiful area overlooking the lake on which to build an overnight campsite. On warm summer nights, Steward and Blossom planned to camp there and enjoy the sights to behold in this enchanted land called the Yukon.

CHAPTER TWENTY-TWO

The following morning came early. After enjoying coffee with their hosts, Grey Wolf and Rose prepared to leave for Johnathan and Shining Star's cabin. The couple's destination was about a two hour walk from Steward and Blossom's home. The couples said their goodbyes and, with Charlie leading the way, the trio left. Steward told Grey Wolf on their return trip he would not be home, as he was planning a trip to Dawson to visit Bev and pick up supplies. However, Blossom would be there, as she was staying behind to look after the dogs.

The trail was well-trodden from visits between the cabins by the tenants and pack animals. After what seemed like a short walk, Johnathan and Shining Star's cabin came into view. Chase, the couple's beloved husky, barked out a warm greeting. Charlie, wanting to be friends with everyone, captured Chase's attention immediately. Grey Wolf shouted out a greeting to whoever was in the cabin.

Johnathan opened the cabin door with his rifle in hand, asking the strangers to identify themselves. Grey Wolf announced himself and Rose, with Johnathan immediately setting his rifle down, no longer suspicious of these intruders.

He invited the couple into his cabin, now excited at meeting these extended family members.

Johnathan introduced his wife, Shining Star, and their child, Grey Eagle. The two couple's embraced, hoping this would be the start of a new friendship. Grey Eagle took a shining to his cousin Rose, wanting to sit on her lap, looking for her undivided attention. Rose loved children and hoped someday she would have a child of her own. The two couples sat around the kitchen table drinking coffee. Conversation flowed freely, as the couples started to get to know one another.

Johnathan extended an invitation to Grey Wolf and Rose to spend the night, which they graciously accepted. He told Grey Wolf and Rose they would eat venison for dinner, as he had shot a young doe yesterday. He had smoked half of the venison, and the rest of the meat would be cooked tonight on the woodstove.

Chase and Charlie returned home; the two dogs having disappeared into the forest two hours ago to hunt for small game. Charlie was the victor, carrying home a rabbit in his mouth. The men went outside to look at Johnathan's sled dogs. He was now the proud owner of six strong huskies, in addition to the family pet, which he used to pull his dogsled during the winter. He had previously borrowed dogs from Steward for the winter months, but decided last year to begin building his own team.

After giving attention to his canines, Johnathan pointed out the lake his cabin sat on to Grey Wolf. Like other wilderness lakes in the area, the water was deep with a rocky bottom. Johnathan told Grey Wolf there were wetlands separate from the lake, where a healthy population of muskrat and beaver lived, their fur coats keeping these mammals warm during the winter.

The men returned to the cabin, where the women were cleaning vegetables they had gathered from Shining Star's garden. Served with the venison, it was a dinner the two couples were looking forward to. Charlie and Chase would also enjoy a good meal, along with Roscoe, Johnathan's resident fox who lived in a den the animal had dug under the cabin. The dogs were lucky the venison had to be eaten or it would spoil. Having no refrigeration during the summer months worked well for the dogs, who were not often given choice cuts of meat to eat. Sometimes good things do happen in the Yukon.

CHAPTER TWENTY-THREE

The mid-August day was warm and sunny. Johnathan and Shining Star were planning to eat dinner with Grey Wolf and Rose around the campfire. As the afternoon turned into evening, the men, with Charlie and Chase in tow, left the cabin to start the outdoor fire. This left Grey Eagle with Shining Star and Rose, who were cooking the deer meat and vegetables. When they were finished cooking, the women joined the men outside.

The campfire crackled, sending hot embers of wood into the evening sky. Johnathan told Grey Wolf about the fall hunt friends and family who lived in the forest had together in late November. Most often, this hunt resulted in the harvesting of large game animals, typically moose and deer. These animals were butchered, and the meat was divided among the families who actively participated in the hunt. Stored in outdoor freezers, the bounty eased everyone's worries over food during the winter.

Since Grey Wolf and Rose were part of the family, they would be invited on this year's hunt. Johnathan told Grey Wolf plans were still in the works for this event, as the number of people involved keeps growing. They were thinking of holding the hunt at Jason and Wendy's cabin, as they would be able to provide enough warm places to sleep everyone comfortably, including the family dogs. Johnathan said someone would keep Rose and Grey Wolf informed of when the hunt would be taking place. Grey Wolf thanked Johnathan for the invitation, saying Rose and he would be happy to attend.

Shortly after this conversation, Shining Star and Rose carried out the food and they, along with Grey Eagle, joined the men at the campfire. The sky had darkened, as the day's light faded. The warm glow of the fire raised the spirits of these forest dwellers, as they made their journey through a life they had chosen and called their own. It was a spiritual journey, provided by nature, in this savage land where survival was not guaranteed.

The full moon rose above the horizon, shining down on Johnathan's campfire. The young couples ate their food in silence, listening to the sounds of nature. The howl of a lone wolf, searching for its pack, and the call of a loon, across the silent lake, were two examples of the beautiful night noises the two couples enjoyed. The low burning coals of the campfire signalled the end of an enjoyable day together. A new friendship had been forged, which would last a lifetime for these two young couples whose lives belonged in the Yukon. It was a friendship cemented by faith and a trust in nature, in a land they called God's country.

CHAPTER TWENTY-FOUR

The following morning, Grey Wolf and Rose prepared to leave Johnathan and Shining Star's cabin, planning to return to Steward's home today. Kind farewells were exchanged between the two couples before the trio headed down the trail. After an uneventful two-hour trip, Steward and Blossom's cabin came into view. Charlie ran to greet Blossom, who was standing at the open cabin door. She was glad to see Charlie, reaching down and patting his head lovingly. Blossom invited Grey Wolf and Rose inside. Charlie hadn't waited for an invitation and was already inside, having barged his way past Blossom.

The friends and neighbours sat down for coffee. Blossom told Grey Wolf and Rose, Steward had left at daybreak for Dawson City. Dawson was a two day walk from here and Steward was expected to be gone a total of six days. He was planning on picking up Omar, the senior pack animal who lived in Bev's barn. He would use him to pack in supplies to the cabin. He also needed Omar's help to move wood from the bush to his homestead. When that work was finished, Steward and Blossom would take Omar to his rightful owners, Jason and Wendy.

Blossom invited Grey Wolf and Rose to spend the night. Rose told Blossom they appreciated her generous offer, but were ready to go home. Even Charlie was ready to get back to his favorite spot, curled up by the woodstove. The couple retrieved their canoe, loading Charlie, the navigator, into the front of the craft first. Grey Wolf and Rose stepped in last and with a gentle push from Blossom, the canoe was on its way across the lake. Blossom, standing on the shoreline, waved goodbye to Grey Wolf and Rose, yelling at the couple they were welcome to return and visit any time.

The lake was quiet, except for the occasional quaking from the ducks who called this lake home. Rose suggested to Gray Wolf they could shoot a couple ducks for dinner, since they had no food at their cabin. Grey Wolf told Blossom that was a good idea, and he would harvest two ducks from their lake when they were closer to home.

After an hour, the couple found themselves in the channel separating Steward's lake from theirs. Another hour in the canoe and they would be home. As the couple moved from the channel into their lake, two noisy Mallard ducks flew overhead and landed in the water nearby. Grey Wolf picked up his rifle, ready to seize on this opportunity for an easy dinner. Two shots from his gun upended the plans of these once healthy ducks.

Rose paddled over to where the birds lay in the water. Grey Wolf reached over the side of the canoe, pulling the birds from the water and putting their still bodies on the floor of the boat. An hour later, Charlie barked with his tail wagging. He had seen their cabin. The dog knew in a short time he would be out of this canoe and dozing comfortably by the woodstove. Grey Wolf and Rose felt the same way, planning to join Charlie for an afternoon nap. The couple were happy to be home and were looking forward to sleeping in their own bed, in their cabin in the woods.

CHAPTER TWENTY-FIVE

Grey Wolf and Rose maneuvered the canoe toward the shoreline which faced the cabin. Before the craft touched land, Charlie jumped from the canoe, sniffing his way toward the cabin. Upon reaching the door, he turned to see what Grey Wolf and Rose were doing. The couple had unloaded the canoe and were pulling the craft from the water, placing it among the evergreen trees where it was stored. They picked up their personal belongings from the shoreline, leaving the ducks Grey Wolf had shot to be retrieved later.

The couple walked toward a waiting Charlie, whose tail was wagging. Grey Wolf opened the cabin door, and the trio entered their home. The inside of the structure was damp and cold, prompting Rose to start a fire in the woodstove. Soon, the interior of the cabin was warm in both temperature and human spirit. Rose made coffee, while Grey Wolf went to retrieve the ducks he had left on the shoreline.

When he arrived at the lake, a surprise awaited Grey Wolf; the two mallards he had shot were gone. Grey Wolf scratched his head in disbelief at the theft and briefly mourned the loss of the couple's dinner. He surmised it must have been any one of a few different animals that walked off with his ducks. Disappointed Grey Wolf turned and walked back to the cabin.

After telling Rose what happened, he said he had learned a lesson and was sorry that because of his mistake they would go hungry tonight. Rose helped solve this problem, suggesting that she and Grey Wolf take the canoe and catch fish for dinner. The couple were hungry, and fish was readily available when using their net.

The trio left their cabin to retrieve the canoe and soon found themselves surrounded by water and forest. The tranquillity the couple felt while paddling on the lake was overwhelming, as they took in nature's gift to mankind. Within a brief time, Grey Wolf and Rose had caught enough fish for dinner. They turned the canoe around and paddled back to shore. Grey Wolf headed off to clean the fish while Rose went to gather some potatoes from the garden.

Charlie, smelling the raw fish, woke up from his sleep and followed Grey Wolf out to the shed to see what he could scrounge from the remains of the fish. Charlie enjoyed eating the innards of the fish, finding these remains tastier than when the meat was cooked and fed to him at dinner.

Soon, the smell of cooking fish filled the cabin, the hungry residents waiting for Rose to put dinner on the kitchen table. Charlie positioned himself beside Rose as they began to eat, knowing she would give him more scraps than he would receive from Grey Wolf. Life for Grey Wolf and Rose was good. The coming winter would be the couple's first big challenge as they navigated the ways of living alone in the north, a true test of survival in this untamed land called the Yukon.

CHAPTER TWENTY-SIX

Another summer in the Yukon was nearly over as the calendar changed to September. The signs of autumn were now readily visible and would eventually take over the landscape. The trees' foliage was in the process of becoming a coat of many colours, before falling to the ground. Grey Wolf and Rose had one more cabin they wanted to visit before winter, Jason and Wendy's. Wendy was one of Bev's favorite family members. Wendy thought of this woman more as an adoptive mother than an aunt. When Grey Wolf and Rose were at Bev's on one of their visits, they had met Jason and Wendy, their son, Kuzih, and the family dog, King. At that time, Jason invited the couple to visit their cabin sometime in the future. Today, the couple was taking them up on their offer.

With Charlie travelling so well in the canoe, a journey like this was brief, usually with no complaining on the dog's part. Grey Wolf and Rose planned to canoe to Steward and Blossom's home first. After a short visit with the couple, they would continue their journey, walking two hours to Jason and Wendy's cabin. While visiting Jason, Grey Wolf hoped to discuss the upcoming hunt.

The day was sunny and warm with little breeze, perfect for canoeing. The craft slid gracefully across the blue waters of the pristine northern lakes. The couple were silent, only the occasional whine from Charlie broke the stillness in the air. After a pleasant trip across two lakes, Steward's cabin came into view. Grey Wolf and Rose beached their canoe on the shoreline the cabin sat on. They were met with a chorus of barking from Steward's sled dogs and his one sled dog came running to greet them. This particular dog was extremely friendly and often allowed off leash to roam the property.

Grey Wolf noticed Steward and Blossom's canoe was not in its usual resting place. He scanned the horizon and surmised they were on the lake fishing. He and Rose would leave their canoe on the beach and the trio would continue their journey to Jason and Wendy's cabin. The sled dog followed Charlie for thirty minutes, before realizing he was not welcome on this trip. Finally, the husky turned around and went home disappointed.

The trail to Jason and Wendy's place was well marked. On the journey, Grey Wolf and Rose came across a scenic overhang, which was a beautiful area to stop and rest. As they were sitting on a couple of rocks, they realized it was a gorgeous spot to enjoy the spectacular scenery, including that of a lake which surrounded them. A short time later, Grey Wolf and Rose reached a creek with a well-worn path along its bank. Following this trail for thirty minutes, led them directly to Jason and Wendy's cabin.

Upon arrival, the first thing Grey Wolf and Rose noticed was the beautiful garden Wendy had grown. Bev had said

Wendy possessed a harmonious relationship with nature and was rewarded with a special gift for growing plants and vegetables. With a small root cellar, which was constructed when the cabin was built, Wendy was able to store her harvest of vegetables in the late fall. Under the warmer cabin floor, accessible through a trap door, the couple could store enough vegetables without them freezing, to eat until Christmas. It was another ingenious idea to make eating more enjoyable in a land which offered little.

CHAPTER TWENTY-SEVEN

Grey Wolf yelled out a greeting to Jason and Wendy. A barking dog could be heard, the noise originating from inside the cabin. The door of the structure opened, allowing King, the family dog, to come bounding out. He ran straight to Charlie, a newfound friend he had once met at Bev's home. With a friendly greeting, Grey Wolf and Rose were invited into Jason and Wendy's cabin.

Jason told Grey Wolf and Rose they were pleasantly surprised they had come to visit, as having people drop by your cabin was not a common event when living in a wilderness setting. Wendy prepared coffee for herself, Jason, and their company. The men talked about the upcoming winter, and the moose hunt Grey Wolf would be participating in. In the latter part of November, relatives and friends living in cabins in the forest met for a social gathering and an annual hunt, which usually resulted in a moose being shot and butchered for its meat. An occasional deer or two were typically also added to the mix, with the food being divided between the families living in the bush and stored in their outdoor freezers.

These freezers were typically dug into the ground, with

a secure entrance to keep predators, such as wolverines, from stealing the meat. The underground storage space was usually situated close to the cabin, where it was easier to hear any suspicious activity going on outside.

The women went outside to have a look at Wendy's garden and the bountiful harvest of fresh vegetables she magically grew in the middle of the forest. Wendy talked about her son, Kuzih, to Rose, jokingly saying the child had grown so fast he would soon be helping his father with the dogs and the trapline. The women shared a laugh together over this comment.

Jason asked Grey Wolf if he wanted to accompany him to see his sled dogs. Like Johnathan, his team was a recent acquisition, having borrowed dogs from his brother-in-law, Steward, in the past. Following Jason outside, it was a short walk to where the huskies were chained and living in primitive dog shelters. On cold, clear winter nights, the huskies preferred sleeping outside in the snow. The shelters were used by the dogs during adverse weather conditions, when they needed protection from the elements.

Grey Wolf noticed how healthy and strong Jason's dogs looked, probably because of the fine care and respect Jason showed his dogs. Jason and Wendy had built a fine homestead here. The couple had built an addition onto the cabin before Kuzih was born, and the outbuildings were improved, giving Jason a well-equipped shed, where he worked on tanning the hides he trapped during the winter. Grey Wolf could understand why the celebration and hunt would be held at Jason and Wendy's cabin. The property and buildings could accommodate many people comfortably.

The men returned to the cabin, discussing with their wives what they would eat for dinner. Jason had both smoked venison and lake trout available. An invitation to stay overnight had been offered earlier to Grey Wolf and Rose, which they had happily accepted. After eating dinner, the two couples enjoyed spending time together, until the quiet of the night sent their tired souls to bed. The magic of the Yukon was on full display, strengthening a friendship which could not be found elsewhere.

CHAPTER TWENTY-EIGHT

Grey Wolf and Rose woke to the sound of honking geese. During the month of September, the geese gather in larger numbers. These flocks travel from lake to lake, feeding aggressively, building up their strength and stamina for their migration south. As time draws near for their departure, additional birds join the flock. Finally, after a grand farewell in October, the birds leave the north for warmer climes elsewhere.

The couples were soon up, enjoying coffee and eating smoked fish. Grey Wolf and Rose were leaving to return to Steward's shortly after breakfast. From there, they would retrieve their canoe, paddle across two lakes, and two hours later they would be home. Charlie and King were playing outside, enjoying the rare company of each other. The time soon came for Grey Wolf and Rose to leave. They gathered up Charlie and hugged their gracious hosts good-bye, telling Jason and Wendy, they would see them in November.

The small group waved as they disappeared down the trail into the forest. Grey Wolf carried his rifle, always aware of his surroundings. Game birds and rabbits could appear at any time on the trail, giving Grey Wolf a chance to procure dinner on their way home. A cool, north wind blew in the faces of the couple, reminding them colder weather was on its way to the Yukon.

After a two hour walk, Steward's cabin came into view. Charlie ran ahead to Blossom, who was outside weeding her gardens. Early homesteaders obtained vegetable and flower seeds from family and friends, allowing them to grow cultivated plants at their cabins. This provided these men and women in the wilderness the ability to harvest a crop of vegetables in late summer and fall, a luxury until the cold weather replaces the green of summer with a coat of white snow. At that time, the diet of these hardy souls will change, with moose, deer, and rabbit, kept in outdoor freezers all winter, becoming their staples. Fish from the lake, game birds from the forest, and meat from the mammals caught in their traps, would round out the early Yukoner's winter diet.

Steward's huskies started barking, alerting him to go see what the dogs were excited about. Upon seeing Grey Wolf and Rose, Steward raised his hand in greeting. He told Grey Wolf, he and his wife were on the lake fishing when they had passed through the day before. Grey Wolf and Rose joined Steward and Blossom in their cabin for a brief visit. Grey Wolf gave Steward an update on the hunt and informed him Jason would be getting in touch to finalize the details of this annual extravaganza. After a short stay, Grey Wolf and Rose gathered up their canoe and Charlie and were soon making their way on the last leg of their journey home.

CHAPTER TWENTY-NINE

When Grey Wolf launched the canoe in the water, he noticed the lake was choppy. The once bright sunshine had disappeared, replaced by a grey, cloudy sky. Grey Wolf wondered if they should cross the middle of the lake to reach the channel which led into the water their cabin sat on. With the chance of a storm rearing its ugly head, they could lose the canoe and their lives. High waves can flip a canoe, throwing the occupants into the cold lake, to an almost certain death. Grey Wolf decided it would be safer to maneuver the canoe around the shoreline until reaching the passage leading into their lake. This route would take at least an hour longer, but it was a better way if the weather was bad.

Having chosen the latter route, Grey Wolf and Rose paddled along the shoreline. A distant rumble of thunder could be heard reverberating across the sky. The wind picked up in intensity, blowing the small craft sideways into the shore. Charlie, in the front of the canoe, whined, indicating his disapproval of the events happening around him. The couple decided to beach the canoe and seek shelter from the approaching storm.

They steered the canoe to a good landing spot on the shoreline. The trio exited the canoe, Grey Wolf and Rose pulling the craft up out of the water, far enough to ensure the wind-whipped waves didn't touch it. After a fifteen-minute wait, the storm moved in a different direction, missing Grey Wolf and Rose's location altogether. Charlie, tired of the delay, had run off into the woods, exploring; his sudden barking caught the couple's attention.

Rose followed Grey Wolf into the forest to see what Charlie had found. The dog was leaning over something lying on the ground. Grey Wolf and Rose approached the dog, surprised at what they saw; bleached human bones littered the area. The skull of an adult male lay leaning against a tree. The trio left the bones where they lay, the couple speculating on what may have caused this man's death.

Grey Wolf and Rose, with Charlie in tow, returned to the canoe. The lake had calmed, appearing like glass, making the rest of the paddling trip home an easy task. After what seemed like a long journey, Grey Wolf and Rose's cabin came into view. As they moved closer to the shore, Grey Wolf noticed a large pine tree had fallen across their front yard. The storm they had avoided, must have moved through the area, blowing down the dead tree with its strong winds. Grey Wolf had worried about this tree coming down on his cabin and was glad that threat was no longer an issue. He would cut the tree up and burn the wood in his woodstove, a suitable outcome for what could have been a catastrophe.

CHAPTER THIRTY

Charlie was the first to reach the perimeter of the cabin. The dog ran to where the pine tree had fallen, sniffing around the downed tree but finding no scents of interest. He left the area, meeting Grey Wolf and Rose on the path which led to their cabin. While walking up the trail, Rose let out a scream. Grey Wolf, who was walking behind her was startled, thinking Rose had seen a bear. Grey Wolf's finger was on the trigger of his gun, ready for any situation which developed. Rose turned and laughed at Grey Wolf. She apologized for scaring him, saying she was startled by a snake which slithered across the path right in front of her. Grey Wolf chuckled, relaxing his grip on his rifle.

Upon reaching the cabin, Grey Wolf removed the extra security from the front door, allowing Rose and their dog to enter. Rose opened the windows to let fresh air enter the building, while Grey Wolf started a fire in the woodstove to take the dampness from the cabin. The couple were glad to be home, and so was Charlie, who was already dozing by the woodstove.

Grey Wolf told Rose he was going to take his rifle and walk the lakeshore, looking for ducks or geese who were either feeding or might fly overhead. This would make it easy for Grey Wolf to successfully shoot a bird or two. He hoped this would allow him to provide a wholesome dinner for his family tonight. Grey Wolf left Charlie with Rose, knowing the dog would be a liability on this trip. Charlie would run ahead, scaring the birds away before Grey Wolf had time to approach them.

Grey Wolf left the cabin, heading toward the lake. He picked up the path that he and Rose had walked many times over the summer, which followed the shoreline. Looking for waterfowl, Grey Wolf had no luck, so he decided to change his strategy and head into the forest searching for grouse. Within minutes of entering the trees, Grey Wolf had shot two Yukon chickens, otherwise known as ruffed grouse. After hunting for another hour, he had two more birds in his bag, for a total of four.

Grey Wolf returned to the cabin, telling Rose about his successful hunt. He asked his wife to start the smoker while he cleaned the fowl in the fur shed. Charlie, hearing the commotion outside, soon made his exit from the cabin, joining Grey Wolf in the shed to see if he could be of any assistance.

The smoke from the smoker caught the attention of two Mounties from Dawson, who were travelling to Grey Wolf's cabin. Their visit was one of two stops the constables would make during the year, to complete a safety inspection. These were conducted to ensure the inhabitants' well-being and the health of their dogs. Trappers in the bush who complied with such an inspection, were rewarded with coffee, sugar, and flour.

Grey Wolf and Rose walked to the lakeshore to meet the Mounties' canoe and say hello to the constables from Dawson. Grey Wolf knew an inspection of his cabin and dogs was imminent but felt confident the men would find nothing wrong.

CHAPTER THIRTY-ONE

Grey Wolf and Rose helped the Mounties beach the canoe, holding the craft steady while the men stepped onto shore. The men introduced themselves as Phil and Bob and explained to Grey Wolf and Rose the purpose of their visit. The couple were more than happy to let the Mounties complete an inspection of their property.

Rose returned to the cabin, letting Grey Wolf give the constables a tour of their homestead. After a walk around the property, Phil and Bob asked to go inside the cabin and the fur shed to look at the woodstove and pipes. The Mounties questioned why there was so little firewood available, it being fall already. Grey Wolf explained the owner of the local sawmill was delivering a winter's supply of firewood in October.

The stove and pipes in the cabin were in fine shape, but Bob pointed out the heating source in the fur shed was inadequate. This infraction was let go with a promise from Grey Wolf these items would be replaced before the start of winter. The Mounties shook hands with Grey Wolf, climbed back into their canoe, and left, paddling out onto the lake. They were on their way to the next cabin, which happened to be Steward and Blossom's.

Grey Wolf returned to the house. He told Rose the Mounties had found everything in order, except for the stove in the shed, which they were already planning to replace. He then headed out to the fur shed to finish dressing the grouse he had started to clean earlier. He placed a large pot of water on the woodstove to boil, as letting the birds soak in hot water for a short time made it easier to pluck them. Grey Wolf had neglected to use this trick on the first bird he had started to clean before being interrupted by the Mounties. Two hours later, the grouse were cleaned, cut up into smaller pieces, and placed into the smoker. By early evening, the meat would be cooked and ready to eat.

Charlie and Grey Wolf returned to the cabin, to find Mary cleaning some beets for dinner, which she had grown in her garden. The couple enjoyed eating both the tops and the beets, as the greens were flavorful and a good source of nutrition. As evening approached, the air temperature cooled. Grey Wolf built a campfire, planning to sit outside to eat dinner. When the colder weather came, the pleasure of sitting outside to eat would be taken from the couple.

The sun was low in the sky when the group left the cabin to eat. The grouse was succulent and juicy, cooked to perfection. The beets and greens were a tasty treat, rarely available to these early trappers who called the Yukon home. Grey Wolf and Rose's log cabin shone in the moonlight like a diamond in the rough, as the campfire burned in the darkness. The love and companionship this family shared was a feeling which could not be denied by this hardy couple of the north.

CHAPTER THIRTY-TWO

Torrential rain hit the cabin roof, waking Grey Wolf and Rose from their pleasant sleep. The dawn's light coming through the windows gave the inside of the cabin an unnatural glow. The couple were awake, listening to the rain falling outside. The air, smelling fresh from the cleansing rains, wafted in through the open windows of the cabin. The couple each felt lucky in their own special way. They had gained independence from their tribe, and they both felt their cabin was a gift from God.

Grey Wolf and Rose had decided, during a conversation last night over dinner, to take a trip to Dawson to pick up commodities such as coffee, sugar, and flour. Rose told Grey Wolf she would like to visit Bev while in town. Bev's greatest joy in life was baking and entertaining her family and friends. She was a gracious host, who over the years had built a reputation for her kindness and honesty. She was a respected woman, loved by the community and everyone she met.

Grey Wolf and Rose pulled themselves out of bed. Rose let Charlie, who was patiently waiting at the cabin door, outside. The couple had decided if the weather was good, they would leave for Dawson this morning. The sky had cleared, the rainy weather having moved on to another location. Grey Wolf and Rose decided it would be a good day to travel. Providing there were no mishaps on the trail, the couple would arrive at Bev's home in the early afternoon.

Grey Wolf boarded up the cabin door, and with his dog leading the way, the group left on their way to Dawson. Charlie loved going on this long walk, where he would chase any animals that wandered into view, sending the frightened creatures running back into the forest with him in tow. Grey Wolf and Rose noticed an uptick in the fall colours which surrounded them. September meant the limbs of the once majestic trees would soon be bare of leaves. Life would not return to the forest until the warm rays of spring sunshine washed over the land.

As the group neared Dawson, their encounters with other travellers increased; men and women coming and going from Dawson for a variety reasons. One such meeting occurred when Grey Wolf crossed paths with an old trapper and his dog. Charlie and this man's dog displayed an instant hatred for one another. Cheered on by his cruel owner, the stranger's wolf dog attacked Charlie. Grey Wolf went to the aid of his beloved pet, telling the trapper to call off his much larger dog or he would shoot him. The man laughed with scorn at Grey Wolf, daring him to carry out his threat. Grey Wolf shot the man's dog to save Charlie's life and then turned his rifle on the old trapper, telling him to leave or he would suffer the same fate.

The man, having no ammunition for his gun, obeyed Grey Wolf's order and left the area immediately. Grey Wolf dragged the trapper's dead dog off into the bush for the scavengers to eat. It was a fitting end for this animal, who enjoyed killing the victims he fought with. Charlie managed to escape the fight with a couple of puncture wounds and some bruising to his body. He would recover from his near-death experience with this savage canine, an encounter he hoped would never be repeated.

CHAPTER THIRTY-THREE

A short while after Charlie's brush with death, the buildings of Dawson came into view. Before travelling to Bev's home, the couple decided to walk to the mercantile and pick up the household goods they needed. Grey Wolf would carry the purchases back home in a bag Rose had made from the hide of a deer. Coffee was the most important item on their list, followed by flour and sugar. Grey Wolf purchased more oil for the lanterns in the cabin and the fur shed and buckshot for his rifle. Soon migrating waterfowl would use his lake as a stopover point to feed and rest before continuing their journey south. Grey Wolf hoped to harvest ducks and geese near the end of the migration. By this time, the outside air would be cold enough to keep the harvested fowl in the outdoor freezer. Rose selected a moose bone for Charlie to gnaw on when he got bored lying by the woodstove. The couple finished their business and continued their journey to Bev's house.

Charlie was the first one to the door, greeting Bev with a big slobbery kiss. She had seen the trio walking toward her home through her open kitchen window. She greeted her company with open arms, welcoming them inside. The smell of fresh baked apple pie permeated the senses of the couple as soon as they entered Bev's house. Apples were in season, allowing Bev to make a variety of desserts with this fresh fruit.

Grey Wolf gave Charlie the moose bone to chew on before dinner. The dog gnawed contently, while lying in his favorite spot near the woodstove. Grey Wolf and Rose joined Bev in the kitchen for coffee and apple pie. Bev said her company always seems to arrive at just the right time; the donkeys' pens needed cleaning again, as they had not been thoroughly cleaned since the last time the couple visited. Bev said the job might be a little easier, as Omar was still with Jason and Wendy at their cabin. He was helping haul wood, which was not an easy job unless you were a pack animal with a strong back.

After finishing their chat with Bev, Grey Wolf and Rose went to carry out their duties in the barn. The donkeys were glad for the company, accepting the wild apples the couple brought them for a treat. Soon Baby Jack would be old enough to work like his parents, packing heavy loads of goods on his back into the bush. Baby Jack wondered if he would face the same life-threatening experiences that his father, Omar, had endured. Every pack animal had nightmares about brushes with death each time they entered their predators' domain, the dark and dangerous forest.

Grey Wolf and Rose worked around the donkeys while cleaning their pens. The two animals were cooperative, moving out of the way when needed. The couple removed the soiled straw from the pens, replacing it with fresh grass from a pile in the corner of the barn. They fed the donkeys some dried clover, which Bev had purchased a small quantity of from the livery stable. The donkeys were usually fed this special treat only when their pens were cleaned, and new straw put down. Grey Wolf and Rose finished their work, saying goodbye to Honey and her offspring, Baby Jack; two lucky donkeys living in the safety of Bev's barn.

CHAPTER THIRTY-FOUR

Grey Wolf and Rose left the barn, returning to Bev's house. Bev was in the kitchen preparing food, a venison stew with fresh vegetables from her garden for dinner and her delicious apple cobbler for dessert. The smell of fresh bread in the oven made Bev's home smell like a bakery. All the tantalizing odors which surrounded Grey Wolf and Rose was making the couple very hungry. They asked Bev if she needed any help, which she declined. Asking what time dinner would be ready, Grey Wolf and Rose found themselves with two hours to kill. They decided to go upstairs to the bedroom and lay down for a nap. Bev told them to go ahead, saying she would call them in plenty of time to make sure the food was hot when they came down to the kitchen to eat.

Grey Wolf and Rose lay down on the soft mattress in their upstairs bedroom. In their cabin, the mattress was made from straw and was not comfortable to sleep on. But Bev's mattress was filled with down and feathers, allowing the couple to fall asleep as soon as their heads hit the pillow. A sudden call from Bev, telling the couple dinner would be ready in ten minutes, broke the silence in the house. Grey

Wolf and Rose pulled themselves from their comfortable bed and made their way downstairs to the kitchen, following the growls of hunger coming from their stomachs.

Bev served the steaming stew, cooked to perfection, and placed a plate of warm bread on the kitchen table. At Bev's invitation, Grey Wolf and Rose dug in, devouring the delicious venison. Conversation flowed freely around the dinner table, when Bev asked Grey Wolf and Rose for another favor. Over the past couple of days, an animal had killed two of her chickens. She had let the hens out of the coop to roam free in the yard and the birds had disappeared without a trace. Bev wanted to get rid of the menace who had obviously learned the birds were readily available, making easy pickings for its dinner. Her chickens were stressed by this predator who wanted to eat them, not a pleasant thought to a defenceless chicken, with only rotting wood and rusty wire for protection. She asked Grey Wolf and Rose to stake out her chicken coop and identify the animal who was making trouble for her chickens. She did not want the animal killed, just scared half to death. Grey Wolf told Bev they would set up surveillance at dusk and try to identify the mystery intruder.

After dinner was finished, the trio retired to the living room. Bev told her company she would be glad when the Klondike gold rush ended, and the town of Dawson took on a sense of normalcy again. Bev told the couple, three men had died recently in a saloon brawl in town, after a fight over money. Too much liquor, too many guns, and rampant gambling were not a good mix for wholesome behaviour.

She told the couple they should be happy they do not have to contend with such craziness in the bush.

Soon the sun was setting over this wilderness, a land the natives called paradise and Grey Wolf and Rose called home. The couple readied themselves for their outdoor adventure, solving the mystery of what animal was stealing Bev's chickens, which their hostess was thankful for.

CHAPTER THIRTY-FIVE

The sky darkened over the streets of Dawson, as the sun slowly went down below the horizon. Grey Wolf and Rose embarked on their adventure, climbing to the top of the barn, using tree branches as their ladder. The couple lay on the roof, waiting for the chicken thief. They listened patiently for any unusual activity. A silence had settled over the forest, when Rose heard movement. The couple watched as a wayward skunk waddled up to the chicken coop, looked inside, and then continued his journey onward, looking for food.

Two hours passed without incident, until the crickets stopped singing and the forest again became quiet. The couple heard an animal approaching from the forest. Grey Wolf and Rose watched as a fox walked out into the open, unaware the couple were watching from the roof. The animal walked around the chicken coop, looking for a way inside. The chickens, seeing their mortal enemy, panicked, squawking loudly in alarm.

Grey Wolf had plenty of time to take a good shot, without accidently hitting a chicken. He fired his rifle three times in quick succession at the animal, the bullets flying so close to its head it took fur from the animal's scalp. Terrified, the fox ran off into the forest fearing for his life. Grey Wolf and Rose laughed at this encounter, knowing the fox would not be in a hurry to return to Bev's chicken coop for a meal.

The couple climbed down from the roof and returned to the house to share their story with Bev. She was pleased with their news, finally knowing who the culprit was. Bev had suspected it was a fox and told Grey Wolf she was happy he did not shoot the animal. Bev realized the fox was hungry and looking for an easy meal, thinking it had worked before, so it would work again. However, the fox was not so lucky this time, and would surely think twice before trying again.

Bev invited Grey Wolf and Rose into the living room for more apple cobbler before retiring for the evening. The couple were looking forward to a good night's sleep, before leaving for their cabin in the morning. The evening was warm, so the couple left their windows open. A hoot owl, using the roof of Bev's home to get a better view of any mice which might be hiding near or around the buildings outside, made his presence known. The howl of a wolf pack in the distant forest made Charlie raise his head and listen. The wolf was Charlie's most feared enemy.

The night passed quickly, with the couple awakening the following morning to the smell of breakfast cooking on the woodstove. Grey Wolf and Rose walked downstairs and joined Bev in the kitchen. She was always sad to see her company leave, and made sure she let them know they were welcome to return anytime. With hugs and well wishes, and a promise to return, Grey Wolf, Rose, and Charlie left Dawson for their return trip home, telling Bev they would see her at Christmas.

CHAPTER THIRTY-SIX

The day was windy and cold, with a stiff northwest breeze blowing. The leaves on the trees were at their peak of fall colours and in just a few weeks their branches would be bare. Mid-September had always been a favorite time of year for Grey Wolf and Rose. When they were children, the changing colours meant winter was drawing near and a blanket of white would soon cover the land. When that happened, life in the forest changed.

The trio had an uneventful trip home and were soon looking at their cabin. Grey Wolf opened the front door, letting Rose and Charlie enter. The cold wind had begun to blow harder, bringing a dark grey cloud cover into the area. Grey Wolf thought it looked and felt like an early snow was going to fall. Shortly after having this thought, a sudden snow squall swept through the area. Large flakes of snow fell, covering the trees and ground in a coat of white. Then, as quickly as the snow began, it stopped. The sun returned to the sullen sky, shining brilliantly down upon the glistening white snow.

Rose started a fire in the woodstove. Soon the crackling sound of wood burning in the stove's belly could be heard.

Grey Wolf exited the cabin to look at the snow outside. Charlie, hearing the cabin door open, followed Grey Wolf out the door. The dog was surprised to see the snow, as he had slept through the squall. He sniffed around in the soft white powder, the new snow reminding Charlie of last winter. Tomorrow, the snow would melt, as warmer weather moved into the area.

Grey Wolf felt pangs of hunger course through him. Neither he, Rose, nor Charlie had eaten since early this morning, when Bev had served breakfast. Grey Wolf suggested to Rose they take the canoe out on the lake to go fishing. Rose agreed, gathering up her fishing net, a valuable commodity that if lost under the water could lead to starvation. There are periods of time for men and women living in the bush, when fish becomes the only protein available.

The couple pulled the canoe from its resting spot and launched the craft into the lake. Grey Wolf and Rose paddled synchronously across the open expanse of water. Migrating waterfowl came and went, stopping at the lake to eat and rest before continuing their flight south. The trees on the shoreline were no longer displaying the green hues of summer, but a cascade of fall colours in shades of red, yellow, and orange. Soon the bare limbs of the deciduous trees would be mixed with the branches of the evergreens, which keep their predominate green colour year-round.

The afternoon was sunny as the couple paddled across the placid blue waters of the scenic Yukon lake. Grey Wolf and Rose steered the canoe to a favorite fishing spot. Rose looked skyward, when a soaring eagle caught her eye. With its majestic wingspan and large size, as well as its telescopic vision, the eagle is the top predator ruling the sky.

Grey Wolf slowed the canoe as they got closer to the area where they were planning to fish. A light chop had developed on the lake, causing the birchbark canoe to bob up and down in the small waves. Rose cast her net into the water, while Grey Wolf paddled the canoe forward. When Rose felt the net getting heavy, she told Grey Wolf to stop paddling and pulled the net into the canoe to remove the fish caught. This action was repeated until the couple were satisfied with their catch.

Today Grey Wolf wanted to secure more fish than what the couple could eat in a day or two. He would smoke some of the fish they caught today, and Rose would fry fillets of lake trout for dinner. The rest, Grey Wolf planned on placing in the outdoor freezer, wanting to see how well it kept. This was nature's natural refrigeration space, used during the cold months of the year to keep food fresh and safe to eat. The outdoor freezer should be okay for keeping fish and small game edible, as temperatures were going well below freezing nightly.

The couple caught so many fish, they stopped fishing for fear of overloading the canoe. Lake trout, living in these isolated northern lakes, can grow up to thirty pounds. These large fish are rarely caught, preferring to stay in deep water near the bottom of the lake. Delighted with their haul, the couple headed for home.

Grey Wolf and Rose had a lot of work to do to prepare all the fish they caught before they could be cooked or stored. Charlie, with his tail wagging, ran to the shoreline to meet the couple when he saw the canoe heading towards home. Charlie knew there was food in the canoe for him. The couple beached the craft and unloaded the fish onto the shore. Grey Wolf threw Charlie a whitefish to eat, which the dog graciously accepted. He carried the fish off to a sunny spot, where he would enjoy the sun while eating one of his favorite foods.

The couple carried their catch to the shed to be cleaned. Rose went inside to stoke the fire in the woodstove, while Grey Wolf began processing the fish. He first cut all the heads off the fish, which was Charlie's favorite, planning to store them for him to eat later. Except for the inners of the fish, which Charlie also liked, the rest of the remains would be placed in the lake for scavengers, such as turtles and minks, to eat.

Smoke billowing from the cabin chimney and the smoker filled the forest. Hungry animals, attracted by the scent of food cooking, would visit the couple's home tonight, including a cunning wolverine who would hide and wait for an opportunity to steal some succulent fish. Grey Wolf called to Rose, asking if she was ready to start frying the fillets on the woodstove. Rose came outside to pick up the fish Grey Wolf wanted her to cook, with the result being a delicious meal they would enjoy eating around a campfire later this evening. It would be a home-cooked meal a still hungry Charlie was looking forward to, hoping to finally fill his insatiable belly.

CHAPTER THIRTY-SEVEN

The evening sky was clear, a million shining stars brightening the darkness of the night. The logs in the campfire crackled, the flames from the burning wood sending smoke skyward. Grey Wolf pulled the cooked fish from the smoker and called Rose to join him and Charlie around the campfire. He asked her to bring a few of the fillets of trout she had fried earlier out with her. Grey Wolf had roasted some potatoes in the hot coals of the campfire to eat with the fish for dinner. Rose left the cabin carrying food with her, sitting on a large rock and joining Grey Wolf and Charlie. It was obvious Charlie had already eaten some fish, but the dog was still hovering over Grey Wolf, wanting more.

Looking skyward, Rose caught a glimpse of a shooting star sending a path of light across the night sky. The sight brought back memories of when she and Grey Wolf were younger and living with their tribe. To escape the realities of their hard life in the wilderness, they would disappear to a private spot they shared together and lay on their backs in the grass. The couple would wait, eyes intensely watching the stars. A flash of light travelling across the night sky was their reward for waiting, a shooting star to wish upon. They shared the belief this would make all their dreams come true.

The wolverine lurked on the edge of the forest, the smell of smoked fish capturing his senses. The animal knew Grey Wolf was armed and would use the gun against him with little provocation. The fox was waiting also, the hungry animal knew the wolverine was close by and did not want to engage with him. The fox hoped the wolverine would get tired of waiting for the couple to retire to the cabin for the night and leave the area in frustration.

Wolverines have little patience, making decisions based on impulse, not common sense. This is why the wolverine left the area before he got himself in trouble. This let Savage, the hungry fox, to allow himself to be seen in the shadows, hopeful for a meal. Grey Wolf and Rose fed him on occasion, and he thought there might be some extra fish left over from dinner for him.

The couple sat around the campfire until after midnight. Grey Wolf let the wood in the firepit burn down to embers. The dark forest surrounding the couple appeared to be without life. The only sound to be heard was the sizzle of the last embers of wood burning to exhaustion. Grey Wolf and Rose pulled their tired bodies from where they were perched on the hard rocks. With the ever-faithful Charlie in tow, the couple returned to the cabin for the remainder of the night.

Having waited patiently for a handout, and receiving none, the fox began to explore the area around the fire. He searched where Grey Wolf and Rose had been sitting, finding a piece of smoked fish left over from dinner. Savage was happy Grey Wolf had forgotten to take this treasure with him when he returned to the cabin. The lucky fox grabbed his prize, running off into the safety of his den to eat the fish he had found.

The occupants of the cabin slept peacefully and would not awaken until dawn, when another day would begin, with the sun rising over the couple's beautiful northern lake. It would be a moment of absolute beauty on display in the Yukon.

CHAPTER THIRTY-EIGHT

The first rays of morning light shone through the open cabin windows. The building was quiet, only Charlie was awake, listening to a deer outside eating. Charlie knew the scent of this animal well, as he had hunted deer in the past with Steward, his previous owner. A low growl came from the back of Charlie's throat, as he wanted to alert Grey Wolf to the deer, but did not want to be loud enough to scare the animal away.

Grey Wolf stirred in his sleep, being easily awakened. He always tried to be alert to whatever situation was going on around him. Grey Wolf opened both eyes and listened. He could hear the hoof beats of what he supposed was a deer in his front yard. He quietly got out of bed, leaving Rose sleeping. He approached the open cabin window, and what Grey Wolf saw triggered emotions not common in the north. He saw the beauty of this animal living harmoniously with nature and not a food source to fill his hungry belly. Grey Wolf returned to join his wife in bed, letting the deer live to see another day.

The sound of a raven squawking loudly from the roof, finally annoyed Grey Wolf enough to get out of bed. He opened the cabin door, letting Charlie outside. He yelled at the noisy bird to shut up or be shot. Periodically this same raven would return to the cabin and irritate Grey Wolf and Rose early in the morning, his loud voice waking them. When the couple had first come to the cabin, Grey Wolf made the mistake of feeding the bird. After he had done this a few times, he realized the pest would not go away until he was fed. This led to the raven returning again and again, even after Grey Wolf had directed a bullet from his rifle over the raven's head. Not wanting to kill the black bird, Grey Wolf hoped his persistent denial of food would eventually send him on his way, never to return. The couple knew this was wishful thinking.

The outside air had turned frosty, with the arrival of a cold front. A gusty wind blew the fall leaves around the cabin, and the October sky looked dark and menacing. The threat of snow filled the air. Grey Wolf thought about Tim, who owned the sawmill, and was scheduled to deliver the couple's winter wood to the cabin. Grey Wolf was watching for Tim, expecting to see him one day this week. His supply of firewood was dwindling and if his order did not arrive soon, he would run out of fuel for his woodstove. This was something neither he nor his wife, Rose, would be happy about.

Later in the morning, the snow started falling and the winds grew stronger. Grey Wolf gathered enough firewood from the porch to get them through the storm. The winds howled all day and night, but left little snow in its wake. This was not what the couple expected to see when they awoke the following morning.

Shortly after lunch, Charlie started barking loudly, announcing the arrival of company to the cabin. Grey Wolf went outside, hoping it was Tim with his firewood. What he saw was a sight to behold, Tim on a barge he had constructed himself, filled with wood. Tim had also brought a means of moving the wood once it was onshore, a cart and a donkey to pull the loads of wood from his barge to the cabin. It was an ingenious idea, thought up by a man with a lot of time on his hands.

CHAPTER THIRTY-NINE

Tim floated the barge and grounded it on the shore which fronted Grey Wolf and Rose's cabin. The couple and Charlie met Tim at the lake front, where Tim introduced his donkey, Jeremiah, and his helper, Elmer, to Grey Wolf and Rose. The donkey stayed with Tim in a secure building during the summer months, assisting with work around the sawmill. This would be Jeremiah's last job for the season in the bush, as Tim was returning the donkey to Dawson tomorrow to be boarded for the winter, in a secure barn out of the wilderness elements.

Tim and Elmer immediately started throwing the firewood off the barge onto the shore. Grey Wolf boarded the boat and began tossing the wood as well. When they finished throwing the wood off the barge, Tim unloaded Jeremiah and a small, wheeled cart from the boat, which the donkey could use to pull the heavy wood. Three hours later, Grey Wolf and Rose's winter firewood was piled by the porch, ready to be split.

As Grey Wolf looked at the pile, he realized it would take a long time to split all the wood. He asked Elmer if he would be willing to return, at his convenience, and spend a day splitting the firewood. As Grey Wolf offered to pay him well for his time, Elmer said he would be back within the next two weeks. Grey Wolf told him to come anytime, and if he and Rose weren't there, to just go ahead and get the work done, giving him a deposit up front. Tim told Rose he and Elmer had to refuse her invitation for coffee, as getting home before dark was a priority. Grey Wolf tipped the men a silver dollar each for the good work they had done, delivering and unloading the firewood. The men left, wishing the couple luck in surviving the brutal winter.

The couple were greatly relieved to no longer be worried about securing enough wood before winter. Grey Wolf split a few pieces of the new firewood to fill the woodstove. Charlie took up his position on the floor beside the stove. The new, dry wood burned well and would provide the cabin with plenty of heat this winter.

Grey Wolf was hungry. He thought about the deer he could have shot, harvested, and stored in his outdoor freezer. He did not regret the decision he made regarding this animal, knowing a greater power would provide his next meal for making the choice he did. As darkness settled over the couple's homestead, Grey Wolf went outside and retrieved the rest of the uncooked fish from the outdoor freezer. Rose would fry the fillets on the woodstove and serve it with carrots for dinner. All the vegetables had now been picked from Rose's garden. A few of the root vegetables and potatoes were stored under the floor of the cabin, where they would stay fresh, and not freeze, for at least another four weeks.

The wind blew through the bare limbs of the hardwood

trees in the bush, their summer foliage now laying dead on the ground. Soon the snows of November would cover the Yukon in a sea of white, as winter would take hold of the land, not letting its tight grip go until the following spring. Grey Wolf and Rose drifted off to sleep, not awakening until the following morning. The new day dawned bright and sunny, a gift rarely bestowed by Mother Nature at this time of year, when hardships were the norm.

CHAPTER FORTY

Grey Wolf and Rose, usually up at dawn, decided to stay in bed this morning. Charlie felt likewise, not wanting to move from his comfortable position by the woodstove, not even for a bathroom break. The quiet of the early morning was broken by a distant shout coming from the lake. This loud voice caught Charlie's attention first, the dog picking up his head, a low growl emanating from the back of his throat.

Grey Wolf woke Rose, telling her they had company. He pulled himself out of bed and looked out the cabin window, only to see the couple's closest neighbour, Steward, who Grey Wolf had been expecting to visit before the end of October. Steward had earlier offered to help rehabilitate Grey Wolf's dog shelters, which were in a state of disrepair.

Charlie was now at the cabin door with tail wagging, waiting to be let out. He realized whoever the stranger was, he was a friend, not a foe. Grey Wolf opened the cabin door to let the dog outside to greet Steward. The men shook hands upon meeting, cementing their newfound friendship even stronger. Grey Wolf invited Steward into the cabin for coffee. Rose had already put water on the woodstove to boil, expecting Steward would enjoy a nice hot drink.

Steward gave Grey Wolf an update on the moose hunt, which he had been invited to participate in this year. The date had been set for the third week of November. The couples were to meet at Wendy and Jason's cabin, where the hunt would take place. The conversation then turned to Grey Wolf's dog shelters, with him telling Steward he had all the materials to complete the repairs. Steward told Grey Wolf today was as good as any to get the work done. Grey Wolf agreed and within a short time the men were busy sawing and hammering lumber.

Grey Wolf was expecting the dog team his father was bringing would consist of six dogs. After four hours of steady work, the repairs to the dog shelters were finished. Steward joked all they needed now was snow for the dogs to pull a sled on. The men returned to the cabin, eating smoked fish which Steward had brought with him. After eating and resting a short while, Steward explained he needed to get home. Blossom had not been feeling well and Steward was worried about her. Grey Wolf and Rose thanked Steward for his help, telling him they would see him at Jason and Wendy's at the end of next month.

Steward left to go home, leaving Grey Wolf and Rose once again alone in their cabin with Charlie. They decided to hike the trail they had started around the perimeter of their lake. The couple would take their rifle with them and shoot any game birds they might see. Charlie would accompany them on this trip, and as luck would have it, Charlie would be exactly who the couple ended up needing on their leisurely trip around the lake.

CHAPTER FORTY-ONE

The bright afternoon sun shone done on this wilderness called the Yukon. The clear blue sky painted a picture of perfection in this land of unspoiled beauty. Grey Wolf and Rose, along with Charlie, exited the cabin for their walk. The couple and their dog strolled toward the forest which bordered the lake. A cold, late-autumn breeze blew across the water, numbing the cheeks of the hikers. The couple found the path, now covered in a carpet of many layers. The beauty in the north at this time of year was profound; the lake surrounded by a forest of trees, most in stages of undress, exchanging their summer coats for winter attire.

The sound of leaves crunched under the feet of Grey Wolf and Rose, the only sound to break the serenity which surrounded the couple. Charlie forged ahead, hoping to find something new and exciting. The dog's path crossed that of a cranky, old black bear who was trying to find enough food to build up his fat stores, helping him survive his long winter hibernation. Grey Wolf was alerted to Charlie's encounter by the dog's sudden, persistent barking, indicating he found himself in trouble. Grey Wolf motioned for Rose to stop and wait.

Charlie's barking drew nearer, as the dog was now retreating, looking for protection from its owner. The couple readied their rifles, waiting for the appearance of whatever was chasing Charlie. Moments later, the dog came into view, being chased by a large black bear looking for dinner. An expression of terror filled Charlie's eyes, as he tried to outrun the bear. Immediately grasping the situation, the couple both shot to kill the predator; two gunshots ringing out in quick succession. The bear stopped running and in dramatic fashion, staggered forward for a foot or two before falling dead on the hard, cold ground.

The couple celebrated their success at saving Charlie's life from the bear. They then realized the animal needed to be harvested for food, with the meat carried the short distance back to the cabin. They could pack the larger cuts to the fur shed, where it would be properly butchered and eventually stored in the outdoor freezer. The cold, outside air would keep the meat fresh, and even frozen, to be eaten as needed.

Charlie was first to reach the dead bear, his cowardice having turned to bravado as he stood on top of the dead animal. Grey Wolf and Rose, with their plans changed, returned to their cabin to retrieve the necessary tools to cut the bear into manageable pieces. These smaller sections of the animal could then be carried back to the cabin, which they hoped to accomplish before dark. It would prove to be a large task for only two sets of hands.

CHAPTER FORTY-TWO

Rose walked the short distance back to the cabin and retrieved the knives she and Grey Wolf used for butchering large game. Grey Wolf went to the fur shed to retrieve the new saw he had purchased on his last trip to Dawson. This important implement in a fur trapper's toolbox could be used for cutting bone, when butchering large game animals, such as moose and bear. The couple arrived back to where the dead animal lay.

Working together, Grey Wolf and Rose soon had the bear gutted. With the omnivore weighing less, the couple used a rope Grey Wolf had carried from the shed to hang the body from a strong tree branch. Hanging the carcass made it easier to work on, when butchering the animal. Rose decided she wanted the hide off the bear, which was in prime condition. She thought it would make a great rug on the cold floor of the cabin.

For the remainder of the afternoon, the couple worked diligently dressing the bear. As Grey Wolf cut large sections of meat from the animal, Rose packed the load to their fur shed. Grey Wolf was scraping the bear hide when Rose returned from delivering her last load of meat. Grey Wolf carefully folded the hide, wrapping it up to carry it home. The bear skin would be stretched and dried in the fur shed, in preparation of use as a rug in the cabin. This was Rose's personal project; one she took upon herself to do. Before leaving the area, Grey Wolf laughed at all the scavengers which had gathered nearby, waiting for the couple and Charlie to leave.

A large crowd of ravens were jockeying closer to the smorgasbord of food being left behind. Savage and his new girlfriend were also waiting. Foxes were typically the first scavengers to reach the scene of a fresh kill, followed by ravens, whose loud calls attracted other forest creatures, such as wolverines to the scene. Within forty-eight hours, any trace of the bear killed here would be gone. Even the animal's bones would be dragged off into the underbrush, missing from where the bear's body once laid. In times of plenty, everyone eats.

Grey Wolf, Rose, and Charlie returned to the cabin. The dog's stomach was full after helping himself to remains of the animal, which had been thrown aside by the couple as they butchered the bear. Grey Wolf had cut two large steaks when butchering the bear in the forest. He planned on treating his wife to a well-earned dinner, frying the meat for her on the woodstove. Grey Wolf appreciated Rose's hard work today and knew she was hungry and tired. He loved his wife, who was always kind and helpful, doing anything she was asked without complaining. After a delicious dinner cooked by a loving husband, the couple went to bed happy. At times, life seemed so easy and problem free in the Yukon, an illusion which cost lives more than once.

CHAPTER FORTY-THREE

The howl of the wolf pack broke the silence of the quiet forest. At night, the bush was foreboding and dangerous. Predators waited in the darkness of the trees for unsuspecting prey to pass. The wolf pack, which had picked up the scent of the bear meat in Grey Wolf's fur shed, wanted to investigate where the source of the smell was originating from. Charlie's keen hearing and sense of smell warned him the wolves were close by and travelling in the direction of the cabin. Charlie growled under his breath, expressing his hatred of these animals. He knew the wolves would come and investigate the scent of the bear meat, but would leave shortly after arriving when they realized they could not make entry into the secured shed where the meat was being stored.

Charlie laid his head back down and soon fell back to sleep. He continued his dream about a new girlfriend he encountered on the trail to Dawson. She was a beautiful dog in both health and stature. In his dream, Charlie never got the chance to met her, as their paths only crossed on the trail. But Charlie noticed this beautiful animal and was certain he was in love with her.

The sound of heavy rain on the cabin roof woke the couple from their peaceful slumber. Grey Wolf pulled himself out of bed, walking to the cabin window. Sheets of heavy rain blew across the lake and the air outside was frigid. Grey Wolf thought it was cold enough for the rain to turn to snow. The fire in the woodstove had burnt down overnight, leaving the inside of the cabin cold and damp. Grey Wolf filled the stove with wood, stoked the embers, and then returned to bed with Rose, who was waiting under the warm blankets for him.

Grey Wolf thought about his father and his promised dog team. The month of October would soon turn to November, by the end of which the lakes would be frozen, allowing dogsleds to travel on their surfaces. Grey Wolf thought this was probably when his father would visit. Waiting for the ice on the lakes would make the journey shorter and easier than traveling through the bush to Grey Wolf and Rose's cabin.

The skies cleared, with the sun making an appearance in the late morning sky. Grey Wolf told Rose they needed to take the canoe and go out on the lake one more time before freeze up. The end of the waterfowl migration was near, with the last of the geese and ducks passing through their area. As soon as the lake froze, the flocks of waterfowl would be further south.

The couple gathered up their rifles and walked to the lake. Grey Wolf launched the canoe into the water and the couple paddled toward the wetlands area of the lake, on the opposite shore. Grey Wolf noticed many ducks had congregated there. Rose paddled the canoe quietly toward the game birds. When the canoe got too close to their feeding area, the birds decided to leave, all flying away together. Grey Wolf emptied his rifle into the flock, taking down five birds with six shots of buckshot. The couple, happy with their harvest of ducks, returned to a waiting Charlie at the cabin.

Grey Wolf and Rose spent the rest of the day cleaning waterfowl and processing bear meat. When this job was finished, most of the meat was stored outside in the couple's makeshift freezer for the winter. However, Grey Wolf had started a fire in the smoker to cook two of the ducks for dinner. He was looking forward to another pleasant night around the campfire this evening, as the couple enjoyed the bounty of food nature had provided them.

CHAPTER FORTY-FOUR

Elmer paddled his canoe toward Grey Wolf and Rose's cabin. As he paddled closer to their shoreline, he noticed smoke floating lazily from the couple's chimney. The grey smoke rose above the trees in the forest and disappeared into the early morning sky. Upon beaching his canoe, Elmer noticed a light covering of snow over the wood pile, which he was splitting and stacking today for Grey Wolf.

Elmer worked for Tim at the sawmill and had helped him deliver the firewood to Grey Wolf's cabin earlier. Elmer had not had an easy life. As a young boy, his mother had died in the family cabin from an unknown infection. Two years later, his father never returned home from checking his trapline, his body never found. What happened to this man is a mystery, which will probably never be solved. Tim took Elmer in under his care and treated him like the son he never had. Elmer proved to be a great asset, working with Tim at the sawmill.

When Elmer had delivered the wood with Tim, Grey Wolf had offered him the job of splitting the firewood and paid him a deposit. Grey Wolf opened his cabin door before Elmer had the chance to knock. Charlie had warned

Grey Wolf they had company, so the couple had pulled themselves out of bed and dressed. Elmer told Grey Wolf he had brought his favorite axe with him to use and would like to get started. Grey Wolf told Elmer he would retrieve his axe, wedge, and heavy hammer from the fur shed and would return shortly to help him.

Splitting firewood was a back-breaking job. The blocks of wood needed to be split small enough to fit into a stove. One large block could be split into four pieces of wood of the appropriate size. The men worked throughout the morning, stopping only for a half hour lunch. They continued to labor into the latter part of the day, working until late afternoon, when Elmer announced to Grey Wolf he had to leave soon before it got dark.

Grey Wolf looked at the dwindling pile and told Elmer he had done a great job and he and his wife would finish. The couple thanked Elmer profusely and Grey Wolf paid him the remainder of the money he owed him, plus a nice tip. Elmer left the cabin a happy man. The Yukon had never been kind to Elmer, and like his parents, his life was cut short.

After leaving Grey Wolf's cabin for home, the young man was never seen again. Tim found Elmer's canoe washed up on the shore of the lake near his home, though his body was never found. The spirit of the north had sent Elmer to join his parents in the afterlife, whose souls would never leave the Yukon.

CHAPTER FORTY-FIVE

Grey Wolf and Rose needed to make a trip to Dawson before winter came; the walk to town would be much easier with no snow on the ground. Grey Wolf needed to purchase a small woodstove and the pipes to go with it, which would eat up the remaining money his father had given him. The Mounties, who visited the cabin earlier in the fall, had condemned the woodstove and pipes in his fur shed. They informed Grey Wolf they were a fire hazard and gave him a written warning, suggesting he fix what could become a serious problem.

While in Dawson, Rose and Grey Wolf planned to visit Bev and enjoy her unlimited hospitality and friendly behaviour. Time was catching up with Bev, as she would turn eighty-four on her next birthday. This was an age most people living in the north did not reach, due to the harsh living conditions they endured all of their lives. Compared to most Indigenous people, Bev had lived a life of privilege, with all her daily needs met. She loved to entertain when family and friends visited and stayed with her. Bev was an excellent cook, who treated her company to home cooked meals and baking. Upon her passing, Dawson and her tribe would surely miss Bev's presence, as would her extended family living in the area.

Grey Wolf, Rose, and Charlie were on the trail to Dawson to buy the woodstove. Grey Wolf knew of a man in town who had made a delivery for Mary and Joe in the past and hoped to secure his services. Although he would soon have his own dog team and sled, Grey Wolf wanted to leave this chore to someone else until he had time to break in the dogs. It would be a struggle with the unknown for Grey Wolf and his new dogs to handle moving a woodstove before the dead of winter. When the snows came, he knew his purchase would be delivered in one piece, relieving him of the stress it would create to do this job himself.

The day was sunny but cold. A north wind let its presence be known, numbing the faces of the walkers. The landscape in front of them looked barren, void of its summer colours. The couple walked in silence and soon were at the edge of town. Bev answered Grey Wolf's knock, announcing their presence. Bev opened her front door with a wide grin on her face, always pleased to see family, especially company that cleaned out her donkey pens. And all the animals Bev loved dearly were home for the winter, enjoying their life in her barn.

The couple and Charlie were invited into Bev's home and served coffee, along with fresh baked apple pie. Charlie was given a venison bone and told to go lay by the fire. Grey Wolf explained his plans to Bev, regarding the stove and pipes he was buying for the fur shed. He needed the man's name who had delivered goods to Joe and Mary's cabin from Dawson. Bev told Grey Wolf the man's name was Jacob and she was sure he would be glad to help the couple out. She gave Grey Wolf directions to the house, but suggested the couple relax and take care of their business tomorrow. Grey Wolf and Rose were happy to follow her advice. They would enjoy a clean bed and a warm atmosphere tonight, comforts not often experienced when living in the bush in Canada's far north.

CHAPTER FORTY-SIX

Grey Wolf and Rose decided to walk to the barn and visit with the donkeys. While they were there, they would also clean the pens for Bev. The wind had strengthened since early morning, the late autumn gusts picking up the leaves and blowing them into a pile against the barn. The excitement among the animals began as soon as Grey Wolf and Rose opened the door. Led by Omar, their welcome song arose for whoever was coming to visit. The donkeys were thrilled to have company, knowing treats would be included. They waited patiently for their turn for a hug, each animal receiving an apple from Grey Wolf and Rose. With cooperative donkeys, the pens were cleaned quickly, the soiled straw replaced with fresh bedding. After finishing this task, the couple bid farewell to the donkeys, leaving the barn and returning to the house.

The smell of cooking and baking greeted the senses of the hungry couple as they walked through the door. Bev was cooking a delicious dinner for Grey Wolf and Rose. Ready to take a break, Bev retired to the living room with the couple to enjoy a cup of coffee. She informed the couple dinner would be ready in thirty minutes. After sitting for a brief spell, Bev returned to the kitchen to finish up her work, while Grey Wolf and Rose finished their coffee.

Looking out the windows, the couple noticed large flakes of snow obscuring their vision to the outside. A passing snow squall was sweeping through the area, leaving a dusting of snow on the ground in its wake. After a brief time, Bev called the couple to come to the kitchen table for dinner. Bev had prepared a hearty moose stew, with potatoes, carrots, and turnips included in the mix. Fresh bread from her oven and apple turnovers, baked to perfection, completed this delicious dinner.

While eating, Bev told the couple her oldest sibling, Mary, was dying. The woman was in her early nineties and had been ill for the past few months. Bev knew her sister's time had run out and she would soon be leaving this wilderness community forever. Rose was saddened by this news but knew her aunt had lived a long and prosperous life.

After eating, Rose helped Bev clean the kitchen. Finishing this chore, the women joined Grey Wolf in the living room for an hour of socializing before heading to bed. Charlie was already sleeping again, after gobbling down the food Bev had put out for him and then enjoying after dinner snacks, begging at the kitchen table.

The night was quiet, only the sound of the wind howling through the bare treetops could be heard. Winter would soon cast a net over the Yukon, making life more difficult for humans and animals alike. The warm bed the couple slept in, and the solitude of the night, allowed for a peaceful and restful sleep for the exhausted couple, a chance to rejuvenate their spirit in an unpredictable world.

CHAPTER FORTY-SEVEN

Grey Wolf and Rose were awakened early by the loud calls of ravens. A few of these birds had found the remains of a dead animal close by and had beckoned their brothers to join them. The resulting fray created a noisy situation in the woods directly behind Bev's house. Curious, Grey Wolf got dressed to investigate the source of the excitement displayed by these scavengers. Charlie, already wondering the same thing, was by the front door waiting for someone to let him out.

Grey Wolf grabbed his rifle, opened the door, and followed his dog outside. The duo headed toward the bush behind Bev's house, where the ravens had congregated. The issue was what Grey Wolf had expected, a wolf pack had killed a deer and fed on the animal all night. Shortly after daybreak, a raven looking for food must have spotted the remains of the animal laying on the forest floor, its blood still a bright crimson red. The canines had eaten their fill, the wolves' gluttonous bellies unable to hold more. Grey Wolf watched the ravens eat; a bonanza of food not expected by these scavengers. This was one of nature's ways of feeding all life in the forest. Grey Wolf held Charlie back, telling him to leave the birds alone. He and his dog turned, returning to the house and leaving the hungry birds to finish their meal.

When Grey Wolf and Charlie reached Bev's, Rose and her aunt were in the kitchen, waiting for an explanation as to why the ravens had created such a ruckus this morning. Grey Wolf told Bev and Rose what he had witnessed in the forest. Bev was surprised wolves had killed a deer so close to her home, which only proved no one really knows what goes on in the woods in the middle of the night. It was an obvious place to avoid, unless you wanted to be eaten.

Grey Wolf and Rose ate no breakfast, as they were still full from last night's dinner. The couple were anxious to get their shopping completed and see Jacob about making a delivery to their cabin in the bush. After a cup of coffee, they left Bev's house to walk into town. They stopped at the only place in Dawson which sold woodstoves and accessories. Grey Wolf purchased the last woodstove the man had in stock; a small, pot-bellied stove he knew would work fine in his fur shed. He paid for his purchase, telling the owner of the store someone would be picking it up as soon as enough snow was on the ground to run the dogsleds. The men shook hands and parted company.

The next stop was Jacob's, a small house in Dawson, where he lived with his mules and dogs. Following the sound of a mule braying, led Grey Wolf and Rose directly to Jacob's home. After introducing themselves and informing Jacob they were Bev's niece and nephew, the man instantly let his guard down. Bev's name was associated with trust in this town, and she sent only excellent referrals to Jacob. He accepted the delivery job, telling the couple he knew where their cabin was located. He had made two deliveries there for Old Joe, the previous owner, who was tragically found dead in his cabin, frozen stiff, yet another sad statistic in this land called the Yukon.

CHAPTER FORTY-EIGHT

After finishing their business in town, Grey Wolf and Rose returned to Bev's house. The couple planned on spending one more night in Dawson before returning home to their cabin. The bright sunshine had melted the dusting of snow the area received yesterday, but dark storm clouds in the distance were threatening to create the same weather conditions again today.

Grey Wolf and Rose spent a quiet afternoon visiting with Bev. She talked about her plans for Christmas, telling the couple she was looking forward to having family and friends stay over for the holiday. This was the usual scenario at Bev's house, great company and good food for at least a couple of days.

After dinner, the couple joined Bev in the sitting room for coffee and dessert. The evening passed quickly, with snow again filling the outside air, leaving a dusting of white on the ground around Bev's home. By the time Grey Wolf and Rose retired to bed, the snow had stopped. A million shining stars replaced the dark clouds, casting their light over the dark forest. Looking out the bedroom window, Grey Wolf noticed there was a full moon. He watched as the moonlight exposed two rabbits eating from the lower branches of an evergreen tree in Bev's yard.

Grey Wolf turned from the window and joined his wife in bed. He cuddled into Rose's back, with his arms wrapped tightly around her. Within minutes, the couple were sleeping comfortably in each other's arms, a sleeping position they would stay in until the first light of the following morning. Bev's call to come to the kitchen for breakfast woke Grey Wolf and Rose from their peaceful sleep. The smell of pork frying on the woodstove stimulated the couple's appetites, making them move faster. Within ten minutes of Bev's yell, they were sitting around the kitchen table eating breakfast.

Bev packed some moose meat for the couple, telling them to enjoy this treat for dinner tonight. When they left Bev's house to travel home, the day was sunny but cold. Charlie led the way toward the path which led out of town. Once on this trail, it was a four hour walk through the bush to home. The first half of the walk to Grey Wolf and Mary's cabin was uneventful, but while sitting for a rest before continuing their journey, Grey Wolf caught movement out of the corner of his eye. He reached for his gun to investigate what had been following them.

Grey Wolf told Rose to hold Charlie while he backtracked on the trail, to try to catch whatever had been behind them by surprise. Minutes passed by in silence, when suddenly a shot rang out, sending a thunderous bang throughout the forest. Grey Wolf returned minutes later carrying a dead wolverine. The unsuspecting animal had lost his life at the hands of the human he was following. The moose meat the couple were carrying had attracted this predator, who had stalked them, never expecting to be ambushed and shot.

Rose told Grey Wolf she wanted the hide from the wolverine, as the animal's fur could be made into a warm scarf for her to wear this winter. The couple left the area and two hours later Grey Wolf was opening the door of their cabin, letting Rose and Charlie enter the structure. He carried the wolverine to the fur shed, where Rose would work on removing the hide later. When Grey Wolf returned to the cabin, Rose was starting a fire in the woodstove; the cabin would soon be warm and comfortable. The couple and Charlie were glad to be home after their trip to Dawson. Life would return to normal for this family living in the wilderness, a normal Grey Wolf and Rose knew was reserved for them.

CHAPTER FORTY-NINE

G rey Wolf and Rose's small cabin sat in the middle of a large forest. Soon the land surrounding their home would be covered in deep snow. Some mammals living in the forest, such as bears, sleep all winter. These animals find dens protected from the elements, and in the latter part of the winter season, female bears' young are born. Nourished by their mothers' milk, suckled in the den, the cubs grow strong. A short time later, the spring sunshine wakes the mother bears, and they take their new families outside their dens for the first time.

The month of October had changed to November. The snows falling one day, no longer melted the next. Soon, blizzards would come to the Yukon, burying the land in snow and the trapping season would begin. The mammals living in the bush would need to hunt for sustenance, which was difficult during the winter. Baited traps, with food they prefer, often drew these animals to an early death. The winter coats of these mammals were sold to brokers and shipped overseas. Once in Europe, the furs were made into coats, stoles, and hats for members of high society.

Grey Wolf was up at dawn. The sky projected a bad omen, with its black clouds and light snow already falling. Grey Wolf told Rose his intuition was telling him the first major blizzard of the winter season was on its way. The couple needed to prepare for an extended stay in their cabin, with extra firewood, meat from their freezer, and water needed to survive a prolonged storm. Survival in the bush required residents to plan for such events, as failure to do so could lead to an early death.

The first blizzard of the season struck with a vengeance. High winds rocked the cabin, the blowing snow creating whiteout conditions. Inside, Grey Wolf, Rose, and Charlie were warm and comfortable. Earlier in the fall, Grey Wolf and Rose had meticulously sealed all the cracks and crevasses between the logs of the structure, which kept all the cold draughts out of the building. The snowstorm blew outside, but the occupants of the dwelling felt safe and secure.

The blizzard raged for twenty-four hours, changing the landscape from brown to white with a foot of new snow. When the storm ended, the door to the cabin was blocked by snow which had been blown against it. Grey Wolf, with his small frame, was able to crawl out the cabin window to remove the snow which prevented the door from opening. During the storm it is important to prevent the snow from blocking the cabin's exit. Opening the door periodically and pushing the snow back from the entrance, helps prevent this unfortunate event from happening. The inability to escape the cabin, can be a death sentence.

Grey Wolf learned a valuable lesson, luckily without suffering dire consequences. Had he not been able to escape the confines of the cabin by crawling out the window, his family may have met with their premature deaths. He took this as a sign his awareness and problem-solving skills needed to improve, or the couple's life in the forest would be short.

CHAPTER FIFTY

The Yukon was now a land covered in snow and transportation via dogsled would soon begin. The movement of goods would become easier, as when the lakes froze, dog teams could run at their maximum speed over the flat surfaces.

Grey Wolf thought about his father, who would soon be bringing his new dog team to his cabin. Grey Wolf was happy he and Rose had caught numerous whitefish this fall to feed the new dogs. The fish were being stored in the outdoor freezer, waiting for the canines to arrive. When he had visited his father, Blazing Eagle had told his son to expect him within days after the first major snowfall. Grey Wolf and Rose were excited about having their own dog team, although their arrival would be a surprise for Charlie, one he may not like.

The sound of dogs barking caught the attention of Grey Wolf and Rose. Charlie was the first to investigate this uncommon occurrence. Visitors were rare when living in the wilderness, especially during the winter. Two dog teams pulling sleds, each loaded with supplies, pulled up in front of the couples' cabin. It was Grey Wolf's father, Blazing Eagle, and one of Grey Wolf's uncles, Black Raven. Blazing Eagle was delivering his son's team and sled to him, a wedding gift he had promised when Grey Wolf and Rose got married.

Grey Wolf and Rose admired their new dogsled and the huskies that came with it. His father had chosen well, giving the couple six fine dogs. Blazing Eagle and his brother, had carried everything needed to spend the night, and would set up camp next to Grey Wolf's cabin. The natives were used to sleeping outside in the cold, and had the items needed to keep warm.

Rose hugged the visitors and invited them inside for hot coffee. Blazing Eagle had carried fresh venison with him, which he gave to Rose to cook for dinner. After drinking their coffee, Blazing Eagle worked with his son to get the dog team settled. Within an hour, the dogs were happy and adjusting to their new home. The men returned to the cabin, to the smell of deer meat cooking. The group were hungry and had settled on having dinner early.

Rose served dinner, venison and the last of her potatoes from the garden, which she had saved for this meal. Over dinner, the family talked about the past and all the hardships their people faced trying to survive in this inhospitable land. The Yukon was no picnic for these people, their survival skills always being tested.

CHAPTER FIFTY-ONE

The morning sun shone down on Blazing Eagle and Black Raven, waking them from their sleep. The night had been comfortable sleeping under the stars, calm winds and moderate temperatures dominating the night. Blazing Eagle and his brother packed up their camp, placing the contents on the sled they would be taking home. Blazing Eagle had incorporated two more huskies than usual into the team, allowing them to pull both men and their supplies. The other dog team, sled, and the supplies it carried were for Grey Wolf and Rose. There were leg traps, which would be useful in catching larger mammals, such as bobcats, lynx, and even wolves. Also on the sled was a large bag of dry food for the huskies, which would help feed the canines when fish and other food was scarce. One of Rose's cousins had asked Blazing Eagle to bring blankets she had made, to keep the couple warm during the cold Yukon nights. Grey Wolf's father had also brought ten pounds of venison, cut from a deer he had shot himself. Grey Wolf stored the meat in the outdoor freezer to be consumed later.

After eating breakfast, Blazing Eagle harnessed Grey Wolf's dogs to the sled. He and his son took the team out to see how the dogs would perform pulling the sled for a new owner. With encouraging words from Blazing Eagle, the dogs did well obeying the commands of Grey Wolf and accepting their new master. A very happy Grey Wolf returned to his cabin in total control of the dogs and the sled.

Grey Wolf's father and uncle needed to leave soon. It was a long journey back to their camp, having to go around lakes and not across them. The ice was not yet thick enough to support a dogsled and its musher. Mushers have lost their lives and suffered the loss of their dogs by being overzealous and going on ice which was not safe. Many dog teams have been unable to escape an icy death when their harnesses became tangled under the water. Mushers, able to escape the frigid lake by pulling themselves out of the water and onto the ice, often perished shortly afterward from hypothermia.

Preparing to depart, the group exchanged embraces of love and gratefulness with each other. Blazing Eagle told his son and daughter-in-law he was proud of what they had accomplished so far and wished them well with their trapping endeavours. Sad farewells and waves were heartfelt as the two groups parted company.

Grey Wolf's new huskies went into a fit of barking upon seeing Blazing Eagle leave. The dogs calmed down shortly afterwards, suddenly liking their new surroundings. The canines knew they would no longer have to fight for food with all the other dogs they were housed with while living at the camp in the forest. Charlie had been investigating his new roommates but was having a hard time getting them to accept the friendship he offered. Grey Wolf watched the rejection Charlie was experiencing from the new dogs, knowing a friendship would eventually develop between them.

Grey Wolf called Charlie to come to the cabin, as he wanted quiet from the dogs while he and Rose had a nap. Charlie ran ahead of Grey Wolf, entering the cabin with Rose. Always the first one to sleep, by the time Grey Wolf made it inside, Charlie was already snoring, curled up by the woodstove. It was the spoiled dog's favorite spot to be when inside the cabin.

CHAPTER FIFTY-TWO

The days of November were passing quickly, as Grey Wolf and Rose had been busy working with their new dog team, getting ready for the trapping season. The annual moose hunt for the families living in the forest was to be held in a few days, with everyone congregating at Jason and Wendy's cabin. Each participant was hoping to fill their outdoor freezers with meat for the winter. This would be the first long distance trip for Grey Wolf and Rose's new sled dogs, their stamina would be tested on this adventure.

Grey Wolf and Rose had decided to wait and start their trapping season after returning from the moose hunt. While waiting to leave, the couple spent the time working on preparations, collecting bait, cleaning traps, and running the trail with the dogs. The couple thought utilizing Old Joe's former trapline was the easiest way to go, as the trail was still visible in the deep snow, and they knew he had been able to harvest a decent amount of furs in the past few years.

Finally, it was time to load the sled for the moose hunt. Grey Wolf and Rose packed as little as possible, saving space to carry a load of meat on their return home. When the couple left their cabin for Jason and Wendy's home, a two-hour journey by dogsled, the day was sunny, with little wind. The huskies, anxious to be going, pulled hard on their harnesses, heads down, with shoulders thrust forward. Initially, Grey Wolf had to slow the dog team down, as Charlie was being left behind. Soon the dogs had settled into a steady pace, one Charlie could easily match.

One hour into the trip, the couple stopped for a rest near an overhang which overlooked the huge expanse of a lake below. Grey Wolf noticed deer tracks traversing the snow-covered lake, which would soon be able to support dog teams, turning it into a superhighway of transportation. After resting for a brief period, the group continued their journey to Jason and Wendy's cabin. Two hours later, the couple spotted smoke, indicating they were almost at their destination. As the cabin came into view, billowing smoke from the smoker and dog teams filled the yard. Grey Wolf was the last of the hunters to arrive. Out of the group of forest families, the only person missing was Blossom, Steward's wife, who stayed home to care for their dogs.

The cabin was noisy and chaotic, full of people who were glad to be all together. Jason decided to start a bonfire so he could move the congregation outside. All the couples had brought a wide variety of meat with them. There were game birds, rabbits, venison, and fish to be smoked, fried on the woodstove or cooked over the campfire. If the hunters shot a moose, it would be on the menu for an all-you-can-eat buffet on the final night of this get together.

Steward had purchased a bottle of liquor while in Dawson, which the men would share around the fire this evening after the women took the children into the cabin for the night. Every available space in the cabin would be filled by humans and dogs sleeping on the floor. Wendy and Jason were thrilled their family was there and were glad this was a party they hosted only once a year.

CHAPTER FIFTY-THREE

Roars of laughter echoed loudly throughout the quiet forest, as the large group of revellers sat around the campfire eating their dinner. The loud, boisterous talk from the men in the group dominated the campfire setting. The wives, not able to get in on any conversation, decided to take their children inside the cabin to finish eating. While in the cabin, they could enjoy quiet conversation among themselves.

The men, loud in their talk, could still be heard inside, making the women smile to hear how much they were enjoying each other's company. Soon, the sound of singing caught the women's attention. After passing around the pint of liquor, with each man taking a drink, the fur trappers had broken into a rendition of song. "Coming thro the rye" was the first phrase the women heard the men sing together. Now it was time for the women to laugh at their husbands, acting like children. Laughs were few and far between in this land of hardships and the wives were happy their men were enjoying themselves by the campfire.

The heat from the fire helped the men to keep their minds off the cold air which was beginning to make them uncomfortable. A lone howl broke the stillness of the quiet night. The men listened, as more howls from a wolf pack emanated from the bush, indicating the animals were on a hunt. Then, as quickly as it began, the howling stopped, leaving an uneasy feeling among the men. Wolves were an unpredictable animal, and the pack could be on their way to Jason and Wendy's cabin after smelling the delectable odours from the various kinds of meat they had cooked for dinner.

The husbands talked about the moose hunt, planning to leave shortly after sunrise. The five men would take three sleds, divided into two hunting parties. If one team shot a moose, they would stop hunting and immediately signal the other men about the kill. Only one moose could be harvested in a day, as the sheer size of a moose made for a long day of butchering and transporting the meat back to the cabin.

Exhaustion set in for the men sitting around the fire. They checked their sled dogs before retiring to the cabin to sleep. Jockeying for a good position, they joined the others on the crowded cabin floor, falling asleep till the first light of dawn awakened them.

CHAPTER FIFTY-FOUR

Grey Wolf and Johnathan were the first two hunters to awaken. The two men got up and let the domesticated huskies out of the cabin. Johnathan suggested to Grey Wolf they should go with them, as the sled dogs did not consider these pets their friends and would act accordingly toward them. Grey Wolf agreed and the two of them took the four dogs down by the lake. The men watched as a brilliant ball of hot fire rose slowly over the tree line, a spectacular sunrise to start the day.

A shout from the cabin broke the thoughts of the two men at the lake. It was Jason, saying everyone in the cabin was up and the men were preparing to leave. The three dogsleds the men planned to take on the hunt were the ones with the largest dog teams. Steward, Jason, and Joe had all volunteered their sleds for the day. The women watched as the men took off, waving goodbye to their wives and children.

The dogsleds left the cabin loaded with happy moose hunters. The sleds moved in a single file, following the trail Jason used for his trapline. At Jason's last emergency shelter, the hunters stopped to discuss their plans. The men decided to split into groups of two, with one man remaining with the dogs. Joe volunteered to stay with the sleds, while the other men put on snowshoes and walked off in two different directions into the forest. As two hours of quiet passed, Joe, who was sitting on his dogsled, began to nod off. The dogs were laying peacefully in the snow resting, knowing they would be working hard again later. The silence in the forest was deafening, putting both man and dogs to sleep.

Suddenly, Joe heard men yelling. The sled dogs rose to their feet, their excitement mounting. Out of the bush charged a bull moose, his full rack of antlers a testament to his size. Startled at first, Joe's instincts quickly took over. He picked up his rife and took careful aim at the giant moose. A thunderous roar came from his gun, the bullet hitting the moose in the side of the head. The moose stopped momentarily, when Joe squeezed the trigger again, this time hitting the animal in the heart.

The moose staggered forward, falling dead in the snow, covered with his own blood. Grey Wolf, who had been hunting with Steward, had come upon the moose in the bush, but had lost sight of him. The moose fled right into Joe's path, who successfully killed the animal with two shots from his trusty rifle. Having heard the gunshots, Johnathan and Jason returned to the sleds a short time later and the group of hunters celebrated as they examined their kill. An animal considered the king of the forest was about to be butchered and stored in the freezers of five families, a fitting end for a moose hunt in the Yukon.

CHAPTER FIFTY-FIVE

Jason headed back to his cabin to pick up the implements needed to cut the moose into manageable pieces. These smaller sections of the animal would then be transported back to Jason's cabin, where they would be processed further. The rest of the hunters stayed with the moose and worked on gutting and skinning the animal.

Upon Jason's return to the kill site, the men worked with the bone saw he had brought from the fur shed. First, Johnathan cut the rack of antlers off the moose, which would be gifted to Grey Wolf to hang over his cabin's front door as a reminder of his first hunt with the family. Johnathan and Joe worked together to remove the animal's head, which would be left on site for scavengers to fight over. After hours of sawing and cutting, the moose was in four sections, each quarter weighing approximately two hundred pounds, an ideal weight for a dog team to pull. The men were ready to load the dogsleds.

Transporting the moose back to Jason's cabin would require four trips. Once there, the meat would be butchered in Jason's heated fur shed, which was large enough to accommodate all the hunters. The men loaded three of the quarters onto the sleds, leaving Grey Wolf to watch over the remaining quarter until Joe and Jason returned to pick it up.

Grey Wolf sat alone in the forest. Within thirty minutes, he saw movement in the trees. It was wolves waiting for their moment to claim the moose remains as theirs. The animals had encircled Grey Wolf and were making their presence known, when the distant barking of sled dogs and men yelling distracted the wolves and drove them back into the forest. Minutes later, Jason and Joe pulled up to where Grey Wolf was standing. They loaded the meat on the sled and headed back to the cabin. After the dogs left the kill site, the wolf pack moved in, laying claim to whatever had been left behind. The moose head, minus its antlers and eyeballs, were a bizarre looking sight in the forest. Joe had taken the eyeballs from the moose to feed to a raven which hung out around his cabin. When scavenging, this was the first body part ravens eat, considering it a delicacy.

Upon their return, the men noticed a gathering of spectators hanging around the fur shed. It was the women and children of the hunters, watching Johnathan and Steward butcher the moose. Rose made hot coffee and served it to the men working in the fur shed. A fire was burning in the belly of the woodstove, warming the shed to a comfortable temperature to work in. Jason estimated it would take the group six hours before the butchered moose could be divided among the hunters.

Freshly butchered moose was sent from the fur shed to the cabin to be prepared for dinner. When the women and children had tired of observing and headed inside, Steward pulled out another bottle of liquor, passing it around to his surprised family members, who were busy butchering the moose. The fur trappers who had gathered for this hunt revelled in their success, knowing this meat would help sustain them over the winter. The spirit of the north had provided for these families, a favor they would not forget.

CHAPTER FIFTY-SIX

The occupants in Jason's cabin awoke early on a cold, cloudy day. The couples had planned to rise at sunrise and pack their sleds for their return trips home. After the men finished butchering the moose last night, the meat had been divided evenly among the five men who participated in the hunt. Each couple would pick up their meat from the fur shed and load it on their sled prior to leaving.

The couples wished one another goodbye, giving Jason and Wendy special thanks for hosting the hunt. Calm settled over Jason's cabin as the company left. The last waves of goodbye were taken as the dogsleds slowly disappeared one by one into the forest. Rose mushed their small team of huskies, while Grey Wolf ran beside the sled. The heavy meat, the couple's personal gear, and Rose were enough weight for the dogs to pull through the snow. Charlie, the couple's pet, was always running behind the sled, trying to keep up with the sled dogs.

After an uneventful trip, the cabin which Grey Wolf and Rose called home, came into view. To their surprise, the couple saw smoke coming from their chimney; someone was using their cabin. A sense of alarm gripped the couple, unsure as to what to do next. Grey Wolf told Rose to hold Charlie, while he approached the building. He cautiously walked toward his cabin, his rifle cocked and ready to shoot if the need arose.

Grey Wolf called out to whomever was inside. A man identified himself in a nervous voice, telling Grey Wolf, he meant him no harm. The stranger opened the cabin door with his arms extended, showing Grey Wolf he was not armed. Grey Wolf entered the cabin, securing the man's rifle to ensure the intruder could not use it against him or his wife. The man said his name was Jack and he had been involved in an accident. Grey Wolf told Jack to sit down and wait, while he called out to his wife. He told Rose everything was fine, the man in their cabin was not dangerous and it was safe to come home.

Once everyone was inside, Jack told Grey Wolf and Rose he lived in Dawson. He explained to the couple, he and a friend were out for the day hunting deer. His friend was driving his dog team and had ventured this way, when his friend had spotted a deer in the distance. Without warning, his friend steered the sled onto the lake to chase the deer, while Jack ran alongside. The lake's ice was thick enough for the deer to walk across but could not support the weight of their dogsled and gear. When they entered the deepest part of the lake, the current had not allowed the ice to thicken. The sled went through the ice, dragging the dogs and his friend to a watery death. Jack had managed to avoid the cracking ice, immediately turning around.

While out on the lake, Jack saw Grey Wolf and Rose's cabin within walking distance of the accident site. The only possessions he had left were his snowshoes and his rifle. Not finding shelter tonight would mean certain death from the elements. Jack said he walked toward the shoreline, where he knew the ice was thicker, and followed the perimeter of the lake until he reached the cabin. Finding the building empty, he entered and started a fire in the woodstove, waiting for the owner's return.

Jack hoped he would not be killed by a suspicious fur trapper, before having a chance to explain his predicament. The sadness in Jack's eyes told Grey Wolf and Rose he was telling the truth. When one fails to follow common sense in the Yukon, it typically does not work out in his or her favor.

CHAPTER FIFTY-SEVEN

Grey Wolf and Rose extended an invitation to Jack for dinner and to spend the night in their warm cabin, out of the cold and snow. Jack was much obliged to the couple, thanking them for their kindness and taking them up on their offer.

Jack told Grey Wolf and Rose he was from Oregon and had travelled north to Dawson in the hopes of going to the Klondike. Strict rules imposed by the Canadian government on men like Jack, regarding the amount of supplies he was required to carry into the Klondike were excessive. These rules made it impossible for Jack to fulfill his dream of finding gold. Jack told the couple he had been staying with his friend in Dawson, when their hunting trip had turned to disaster, causing Jack to lose the only friend he had in Canada. He told Grey Wolf when he returned to Dawson, he was gathering up his belongings and returning to his family in Oregon. His odyssey to the Klondike was a dream he had been unable to fulfill.

Early the next morning, Jack left Grey Wolf and Rose's cabin, planning to walk to Dawson, pick up the pieces of his life, and carry on. Shortly after Jack left, another surprise visitor appeared at the cabin. It was Jacob, delivering the new pot-bellied woodstove and matching pipes. Jacob told Grey Wolf he had passed Jack on the trail here, and had promised to pick him up on his return trip to give him a ride back to town.

Jacob stayed and helped Grey Wolf exchange the stoves. The old stove was carried outside and left behind the fur shed. When the men removed the stove, Grey Wolf noticed the faint outline of a section of wood cut from the floor. Grey Wolf's heart skipped a beat, as he thought about the stories of trappers hiding their newfound wealth in the most unlikely places. Jacob, not saying anything, had obviously not noticed the anomaly in the floor. After helping place the new stove in the shed, Grey Wolf told Jacob he would take care of replacing the pipes with Rose's help.

The two men returned to Grey Wolf's cabin to have a cup of coffee, which Jacob had carried with him from town for Grey Wolf and Rose to enjoy. Jake had also brought a frozen apple pie, given to him by Bev for the couple. Rose would bake the pie in the oven of the woodstove for dessert tonight. After a short visit with the couple, Jacob left on his dogsled to travel back to Dawson City. He would pick up Jack along the trail, saving him from a long trek in the snow.

Once they were alone, Grey Wolf shared the news about what he had noticed under the stove with Rose. The couple returned to the fur shed together, moving the stove off the concealed area of cut wood. Shaking with excitement, Grey Wolf retrieved a sharp implement from under the work bench and pried up the cut piece of floor. In the opening was a small, tin box, which Grey Wolf retrieved. The container rattled when he lifted it, indicating it might hold coins or other loose, metal objects. Grey Wolf and Rose decided to take the box back to their cabin to open. Old Joe's treasure was about to be revealed.

CHAPTER FIFTY-EIGHT

G rey Wolf set the tin box on the table, observing the wax
seal which kept the lid secured tightly. Retrieving his
knife, Grey Wolf broke the seal and lifted the top off the
box, revealing what was inside. He carefully turned the box
over and out of the container tumbled five, twenty-dollar
gold pieces, a large gold nugget, and a deed, showing Old
Joe owned a piece of land in Dawson. There was a picture of
his wife and two children, who were not known to anyone,
except Old Joe. Why he kept this part of his life secret,
nobody knows; it was a mystery Old Joe took to his grave.

Grey Wolf and Rose were happy with the good luck
which had been bestowed on them. Before discovering this
newfound wealth, they had less than a dollar left in their
personal bank. The money was a windfall for the couple,
something they were ecstatic to have in case of an emergency
this winter. Financial stress could now be removed from
their minds, leaving the couple with less worry.

Rose told Grey Wolf she had observed two dog teams
crossing their lake earlier today. Grey Wolf had been working
in the fur shed with Jacob at the time, and did not see the
men or dogs his wife told him about. Rose suggested they

take the sled dogs for a run on the lake. Grey Wolf agreed, realizing he needed to exercise his huskies daily.

The day was sunny and cold, with an icy north wind. Grey Wolf guided the dogs into a more sheltered area, following the shoreline, avoiding the deeper parts of the lake. The snow, which fell the night before, had draped the trees in a veil of white. Rose pointed out the tracks of a fox chasing a rabbit, which were clearly visible. The dogs loved to run across the open lake, pulling hard on their harnesses, their breaths like puffs from the smokestack of a locomotive.

Grey Wolf steered his dogs toward the wetlands area of the lake, wanting to check on the health of the beaver colonies he would trap later this winter. He mushed the sled dogs over the beaver dam and onto the frozen waters of the pond. The couple noticed what looked like little straw houses sticking out of the snow. This revealed a healthy colony of muskrats lived in the beaver pond. A woodpecker, living in a nearby hollow tree, was letting his presence be known. His fast-moving beak sent a distinct knocking sound reverberating through the wetlands.

Grey Wolf and Rose looked and listened to the spectacle of nature which surrounded them. This was the draw of the Yukon, what kept this young couple in this game of survival, in a land which sometimes God forgets.

CHAPTER FIFTY-NINE

The dogsled travelled across the beaver pond. Rose counted four beaver lodges, indicating a healthy supply of beaver in the area, which should assure Grey Wolf of some valuable pelts this winter. As he turned the dogs around and headed in the direction of home, Grey Wolf was happy with what he had found.

On the way back to their cabin, the couple ran into Steward. He felt the ice on the lake was thick enough to run his dog team on and knew his huskies would love to run over the long open stretches of the lake. Running at full gait for an extended period is what the dogs enjoyed the most. Grey Wolf and Rose invited Steward back to their cabin for a visit over a cup of coffee. Steward accepted their invitation and followed the couple home.

Charlie, upon seeing Steward, ran to greet him. He loved Steward and the feeling was mutual. Charlie sometimes missed Steward being his handler, but he was happy with his new life living with Grey Wolf and Rose. After a brief visit with the couple, Steward walked out the door to a brisk wind and heavy cloud cover moving into the area. The Yukon had yet to experience a prolonged blizzard with high winds this winter season. Steward sensed a major storm was coming, telling Grey Wolf and Rose to prepare their cabin and life for what could turn out to be a protracted blizzard. Steward said goodbye, hoping he would reach home before the snow started.

Heeding Steward's warning, Grey Wolf secured his sled dogs and fed the animals. He went to his outside freezer and returned to the cabin with a three-day supply of food. Rose carried in additional firewood, which was stacked beside the cabin. She made Charlie share his space, adjacent to the woodstove, with the wood. The storm gave Steward time to get home before the full fury of the blizzard was unleashed on this untamed land.

Grey Wolf and Rose were comfortable in their cabin, the woodstove keeping everyone warm, including Charlie. The couple passed the time by playing cards and picking up the books they had been reading during the last storm, but never finished. The blizzard blew for two days. Grey Wolf wondered about his huskies, who were buried in the snow waiting for the storm to end.

Early in the morning on the third day, sunshine peeked through the cabin window, awakening Grey Wolf and Rose. The snow glistened in the early morning sunshine, the trees in the forest covered in a veil of white. Grey Wolf rose from bed, dressed, and headed outside to check on his dogs. Upon seeing Grey Wolf, the dogs barked in excitement. The animals were hungry and were waiting to be fed.

Grey Wolf gave his dogs extra whitefish, which the animals graciously accepted. He returned to the cabin, leaving Charlie outside to play in the snow, one of his favorite pastimes. Grey Wolf crawled back in bed with his wife, wrapping her tightly in his arms, and drifted off into a peaceful sleep. The call of the Yukon would keep this couple in the north for life, a life they dreamed could not be found elsewhere.

CHAPTER SIXTY

The blizzard had pushed back Grey Wolf's plan to set their trapline. As it was already the end of the first week of December, the couple decided to wait to place their traps until after the Christmas holiday. The couple spent the next two weeks completing various chores around their home. They broke the trail, exercising the dogs and watching for animal sign along the trapline. Rose successfully set rabbit snares in a stand of evergreens, catching more than a dozen, which were cleaned and placed in the outdoor freezer.

Grey Wolf and Rose woke at daybreak, with a plan to set their fishing net under the ice for the first time this season. After harnessing the dogs and loading the sled with the needed supplies, they ventured onto the ice, heading to one of the deepest parts of the lake. With confidence, they lowered their net through the holes Grey Wolf had cut, and within two hours, had twenty-four whitefish and lake trout laying on the ice. Having been on the ice long enough, the couple headed toward home, happy with their catch.

Returning home, the couple worked together putting the dogs away. Grey Wolf carried the fish to the fur shed, while Rose stoked the fire in the cabin. He started a fire in the pot-bellied stove, wanting to heat the shed before cleaning the fish. He then returned to the cabin, joining his wife at the table while they waited for the kettle to boil. Christmas would soon be here, and the couple needed to plan their trip to Bev's house in Dawson. Without warning, a knock came to the cabin door. Startled, Grey Wolf stood up and went to the door, asking the person on the other side to identify themselves. It was Grey Wolf's father, Blazing Eagle.

Grey Wolf opened the door and hugged his father tightly. Blazing Eagle told Grey Wolf and Rose he was thinking of purchasing a dog team from a man in Dawson who was leaving town. He wanted to run the dogs, in order to judge their performance before finalizing the sale. Wanting to see his son and daughter-in-law before Christmas, Blazing Eagle took this opportunity for a visit. He joined the couple for coffee, and after a thirty minute visit went on his way, happy with what would soon be his new dog team.

Grey Wolf watched as his father mushed the dogsled back to Dawson. This would be the last time Grey Wolf would see his father. While hunting with other men from his tribe in the spring, Blazing Eagle struck off on his own. Preferring to hunt by himself, rather than with a partner, he came upon a sleeping mother bear and her young cub. Unfortunately for Blazing Eagle, the encounter did not end well. The rest of the hunting party found Blazing Eagle dead, mauled by the bear who was protecting her cub.

The couple learned of the tragic death after they returned home from a supply run to Dawson in late April. Grey Wolf's uncle, Black Raven, came to the couple's cabin to tell them about the unfortunate incident resulting in Blazing Eagle's death. Finding no one home, Black Raven left a note, but Grey Wolf did not receive the message until after the funeral had taken place. Missing his father's burial was something Grey Wolf deeply regretted, but he would always carry wonderful memories of living in the wild with his father.

A few days after Blazing Eagle's visit, the couple left for Dawson. Dogsleds were tethered in Bev's yard when Grey Wolf and Rose arrived with Charlie. The couple were greeted at the door by the revellers who had already gathered at Bev's home. Bev was happily preparing Christmas Eve dinner for her company, with Wendy's help.

This year, Steward and Blossom were able to attend this event, having left their two youngest dogs at Tim's cabin. Steward's friend, who owned the sawmill, had purchased three huskies from Steward earlier in the year. At that time, he agreed to watch Steward's dogs at Christmas, if he delivered the canines to his cabin. Steward would retrieve his two huskies from Tim after returning home from Dawson.

A new year would soon sweep across this frozen north. The fur trappers would work on their traplines with vigor, gathering enough fur during the winter to pay for next year's supplies. Over the frigid months, these outdoors men and women would need to procure enough money to pay for any food items, household goods, and ammunition needed throughout the year. Nature's gift of fur to these hardy souls was a prerequisite for their survival in this untamed wilderness, a land where only the hardy survived, a land called the Yukon.

CHAPTER SIXTY-ONE

The group of family and friends sat around Bev's kitchen table with conversation flowing freely as dinner was served. Bev had cooked a variety of meats and root vegetables saved from her garden. Potatoes, carrots, turnips, parsnips, rutabagas, and beets had been stored in the root cellar of Bev's basement, which would last into the month of January. Because such produce was a luxury for Bev's guests' hungry pallets at this time of year, she had prepared an abundance of them to serve everyone around the dinner table. Bev topped off this delicious meal with fresh baked apple pie for dessert, served with coffee.

After dinner, the men retired to the sitting room while the women cleaned up the kitchen. Bev's Christmas tree sat in the corner, reflections from the foil on the tree sparkled in the low light of the oil lamps. Homemade ornaments, donated throughout the years, hung from the tree's branches, making it one of the best dressed trees in town.

The sled dogs outside began barking loudly with alarm. When Jason and Steward rushed outside to investigate the continuous yapping, the men saw something they had never seen before in the Yukon. Looking up at an outcropping which overlooked the sled dogs, the two men saw a cougar. The majestic animal was clearly visible in the moonlight, studying the dogs below. The men watched as the predator turned and walked back into the forest. It was rare to see this mammal in the Yukon, as it was a predator who kept to itself and was seldom seen by humans.

Jason and Steward returned to the house, telling everyone about their encounter with the cougar. Bev said in all the years she had lived on this property, it was only the second time she can remember a cougar being seen. These big cats scared Bev and she hoped the feline would not come back for another visit.

The group sat in the living room conversing into the late evening. Bev was the first to retire to bed, as she was always the first one up, working in the kitchen preparing breakfast. This meal would be followed later by a much smaller dinner on Christmas Day. Bev was serving duck, grouse, and smoked salmon for the main course, accompanied by potatoes, carrots, and turnips, with fresh baked bread. Pumpkin pie, baked in Bev's oven along with apple strudel, would be served for dessert.

The women with children were the next to turn in, followed by their husbands and the rest of Bev's visitors a short time later. The living room was silent as the those still awake listened to an owl hooting for his mate. The wind howled through the bare branches of the forest trees. The squirrels' nests swung dangerously in the upper branches of the large deciduous trees. The animals inside slept peacefully, as their homes rocked like a cradle, back and forth in the wind. This was the lure of the Yukon for the people who lived here, a peaceful place they called God's country.

CHAPTER SIXTY-TWO

Bev stood at the bottom of the stairs, ringing bells to wake her company. When they heard the sleigh bells, everyone was reminded it was Christmas morning. The excited children knew there were gifts for them under Bev's Christmas tree. Within thirty minutes, everyone was awake, dressed, and eating breakfast downstairs in the kitchen. A generous helping of eggs, potatoes, and fried pork was on the menu.

After breakfast, the group of family and friends moved into the living room to exchange gifts and stories of past Christmases at Bev's home. The children opened their gifts from their parents, along with one present each from Bev. Because of the large number of adults present, as in year's past, they had drawn names for a gift exchange. However, Bev received gifts from each of the families present, as a way for them to express their gratitude for her hospitality, not only at Christmas but throughout the year. The adults had also brought one hand-crafted ornament from each family to be hung on the tree, a tradition Bev started a long time ago. The hand-made creations were hung on the tree as a remembrance to Bev's late husband, whom she still missed dearly.

The rest of the day passed quickly, with the women helping Bev prepare dinner in the kitchen while the men took the two children, Kuzih and Grey Eagle, out for a donkey ride. It was a bright, sunny day and all the parties involved in this adventure enjoyed being out in the fresh northern air. The group walked to Bev's barn and brought Omar and Honey out of their pens. The men put the children on the animals' backs, with one man holding onto each child, while another led the animals. Fun was had by all, including the donkeys. When returned to their stalls in the barn, Omar and Honey were each given a special treat for being so cooperative. The children loved riding the donkeys and the mothers laughed when the boys and their dads told them about their experience.

Dinner was served, filling the hungry stomachs of the group seated around the kitchen table. Unfortunately, this would be Bev's last Christmas for entertaining family and friends. The happy Christmas revellers ate dessert and passed the afternoon away socializing together. It would be another year before they found themselves all together again. Tomorrow, all the families, their children, and dogs would leave for their cabins. The Christmas season would be over, and the busiest part of the trapping season would begin for these wayward trappers in the bush.

The twinkling stars shone down on Bev's home, an oasis of peace and comfort in an otherwise inhospitable land. The couples slept peacefully in their beds, dreaming of the happy Christmas that had just taken place. Memories of Bev's past Christmas dinners would fill her family with joy. She was a woman, tough in spirit, whose soul could not be replaced, a true legend of the north.

CHAPTER SIXTY-THREE

Bev's company left the morning of the day after Christmas. One by one, the dogsleds departed Bev's home in Dawson, each carrying members of Bev's family to their cabins in the bush. Grey Wolf and Rose were anxious to get home, as the couple wanted to set their trapline. A pile of fifteen traps were waiting for them in the fur shed, which they planned to set along Old Joe's trapline.

The day was sunny with calm winds, as the dogsled moved forward, with Charlie running behind. The dog was trying to keep up with the team pulling the sled. The spray from the snow off the skis of the sled and the steam from the huskies breath clouded the clear northern air. Grey Wolf steered the dogsled onto a lake, which was a shorter route than the one they used when walking to and from town. Once they crossed this expanse of water, the couple would almost be home.

The huskies ran faster over the ice and snow, as the open surface allowed them to build up more speed. By the time the team reached the far shore, Charlie was a quarter mile behind them. Grey Wolf steered the dog team off the lake, picking up the short trail which led to home. Stopping the sled in front of the cabin, he removed the board from across the front of the door so the couple could enter the building. The cabin's interior was cold and damp. Grey Wolf started a fire in the woodstove and soon Rose let a barking Charlie, stuck on the opposite side of the cabin door, into the building. He had finally arrived home, after his lonely run across the lake. After Charlie entered the cabin, he dropped from fatigue by the woodstove. His exhaustion won out over his hunger, as all he wanted to do was sleep in his favorite spot. Grey Wolf and Rose laughed, thinking Charlie was a clown.

The cabin was soon glowing, a bastion of warmth and comfort. The couple relaxed in the security of their home, as a light snow started falling out of the afternoon sky. A fresh covering of snow was welcomed by Grey Wolf, as it would allow him to identify the tracks of various animals living in the area when the couple set traps tomorrow. When Grey Wolf and Rose went to bed that evening, snow was still falling. The quiet of the night and watching the large snowflakes drift lazily by the cabin window, sent the couple into a peaceful sleep, lasting until the following morning.

Grey Wolf and Rose were up with the rising sun. Rose made coffee while Grey Wolf prepared the dog team for their first day of work. The couple planned on setting the fifteen leg traps sitting in the fur shed today. Charlie would stay home and guard the cabin. He was still tired from yesterday's long run home from Dawson City.

The couple loaded the traps, and the bait to go with them, onto the sled and mushed the huskies forward. The snow had stopped before daybreak, leaving the landscape covered in a coat of white. Tracks of animals living in the forest were abundant, as mammals love to explore when fresh snow has fallen. New snow and no wind seem to make these animals' senses more acute, allowing them to be successful hunting during the night. Setting the traps with smelly bait should attract many mammals overnight, if the weather holds.

The dogs worked admirably for Grey Wolf and Rose; they were obedient and got along well with each other. Grey Wolf was happy with his father's choice of huskies, whom he would care for and treat like family. The couple set all the traps they had left with this morning and headed toward home. After checking the trapline tomorrow, Grey Wolf planned to set one beaver trap in the wetlands.

Back at the cabin, Charlie was waiting for his owners to return, as he needed outside to go to the bathroom. His wishes were soon answered, when he heard the dog team approaching from a distance. Ten minutes later, he heard Grey Wolf and Rose talking, relieved they had come home. When the cabin door opened, Charlie scooted right past the couple to go outside. The couple entered the cabin shaking their heads and laughing at Charlie, their dog who lived the good life.

CHAPTER SIXTY-FOUR

The morning sun rose slowly above the horizon. Soon, the sun shone through the cabin window, its bright rays hitting the couple's faces, awakening Grey Wolf and Rose from their restful sleep. Rose was the first one out of bed, letting a restless Charlie outside. Rose stoked the fire, adding more wood, while putting a kettle of water on the cooktop for coffee.

Grey Wolf pulled himself out of bed and dressed for going outside. He wanted to feed his sled dogs before taking them to check his traps this morning. After the dogs were fed, Grey Wolf returned to the cabin to join Rose for coffee. The conditions for trapping animals last night could not have been better, with Grey Wolf expecting a record catch for their first day of trapping season.

Charlie decided to stay at home in the cabin again, as these trips following the dogsled physically exhausted him. He found it impossible to keep up with the sled dogs, deciding relaxing in the cabin sounded like a much better choice.

Grey Wolf went out to ready his dog team. As soon as the huskies saw him returning, they were excited, knowing they were going on a run. The animals loved the feel of the harnesses on their backs, as the dogs pushed their shoulders forward. The synchronicity of the dogs pulling together as one, allowed the sled to glide gracefully across the snow-covered landscape.

Mushing his dogs to the first trap on the trapline, Rose pointed out a dead animal lying in the snow. It was a pine marten, once a common species found in the north, which is now in decline. The couple followed their trapline, and as Grey Wolf expected, a bumper crop of fur was harvested. They collected six fur bearing mammals from the fifteen traps they had set. The most valuable catch of the day was a rare silver fox, its pelt being more precious than that of a beaver.

Grey Wolf had packed an axe on the sled before leaving the cabin, planning to set a trap for beaver today. He mushed his dog team onto the beaver pond, which was at the end of his trapline. He steered the sled dogs close to the beavers' lodge, stopping at what he thought would be the best spot to set the trap. Following his father's teachings, he set the device remembering his father's guidance and hoping it would be successful. Beaver hides were one of the most valuable furs in a trapper's collection to be acquired over the winter.

After finishing setting the beaver trap, Grey Wolf turned the sled loaded with fur toward home. Upon their return, the couple unloaded their day's haul, storing it in the fur shed. After unloading their other supplies, Grey Wolf returned the dogs to their living quarters. He then joined his wife in the cabin to celebrate their successful first day of fur trapping at their new home in the Yukon.

CHAPTER SIXTY-FIVE

Upon awakening the following morning, a grey sky, filled with white snow, greeted the couple. Grey Wolf and Rose had spent the afternoon, and part of the previous evening, harvesting the furs of the animals they had trapped that day. They were both experienced at doing this work, having been taught by Blazing Eagle, Grey Wolf's father. The remains of the smaller mammals would be used to bait the traps. The carcass of the silver fox was treated with more respect, with the remains of the canine being taken deep into the forest, where nature would dispose of them.

The couple needed to replenish their stock of whitefish for the dogs. Today, they would leave their traps be, returning to check them tomorrow. When Grey Wolf had readied the dog team to go out on the lake, he called out to Rose, asking if she was ready. She joined Grey Wolf on the sled, leaving Charlie at home alone again. The late December cold was numbing; the icy north wind blowing across the open lake was frigid. After Grey Wolf had reopened the hole in the ice using an axe, Rose skillfully used her net and easily caught enough whitefish to provide the huskies with nutritious food for three days.

Grey Wolf and Rose were busy during the month of January and throughout February and March. Their daily routines were repetitious, checking and resetting traps, harvesting fur, and fishing for food for the dogs. After significant snowfalls, their routines took longer, as they had to break the trail and dig out their traps to reset them. In the end, the couple accumulated many valuable furs, including numerous beaver pelts, over the winter season.

Unfortunately for the forest community of fur trappers, they received some devastating news in the spring; one night in April, Bev died in her sleep. She would be missed tremendously by the people she loved the most, her family residing in the forest. Bev's spirit would always be there with them, as they fought the feelings of loneliness without her. Life would go on in this wilderness community, as they created a new chapter in the lives of this close-knit family surviving in the bush. This was the way of the Yukon.

ACKNOWLEDGMENTS

I would like to thank my wife, who dedicated herself to the completion of this writing project. Her skills in editing and assistance with producing the finished draft were instrumental. I am certain the publishing of this book would never have happened without her.